BURN SCAR

T.J. Tao

To all of the survivors of the CampFire, which destroyed
Paradise, Ca. on Nov. 8th, 2018.
My friends and neighbors, this novel may be fictional,
but it is our story. Keeping the memory alive,
in tribute to those that did not survive. God Bless.
#ParadiseStrong #RidgeStrong

Chapter One

Power, wielded without concurrent leadership ability, becomes the last gasp of breath for a mutinied Captain intent on going down with his or her vessel. Yes, that is better than a flushing toilet analogy, but not nearly as relevant.

Politics in a small town are far different from the divisive nature of the national political scene. In theory, everyone is doing what they can to better the town as a whole. Which is great until election season... then the people want answers, they want reports of progress. They want potholes fixed and to be able to find a job. They want the town to actually be better. Economic stagnation and decline tend to paint a target on a Town's leadership. New candidates seem to come out of the woodwork to challenge the status quo. And the status quo doesn't like it.

Joanna Moody was pissed. She tossed the file she had been reading onto Town Manager Jillian Dupree's desk with an audible sigh. Mayor Joana Moody was in the midst of an unexpectedly difficult bid for re-election to the Town Council of Genna.

"So, that's it then?", her nasal voice exasperated, "Three weeks until the election and the sewer project is dead?"

Bringing a sewer to Genna had been her primary goal and talking point for the last two years. While the other candidates spoke of fire safety and economic growth, she had focused on past achievements and the sewer which she believed would revitalize the business community. But as this file showed, for the third time, The Ridge was simply not geologically compatible with a sewer system. A layer of slate too shallow under the soil made it a near-impossible challenge and being on a ridge with canyons on both sides added a logistical nightmare that would make the already outrageous price tag double, if not triple. But her can-do attitude and her 30 years at the Idaho Department of Transportation told her she could get this done. She had managed highway projects that ran into geological hurdles numerous times and was always able to plow through and find a way to make it happen. Not this time. She was incredulous.

"Don't give up yet! The voters will sense it if you lose your focus. Sewer or no sewer I need you to be re-elected." Jillian urged. She meant it. She needed Moody to be re-elected.

Genna had a slightly unorthodox Town Council electoral process, not unheard of, but not common either. The title of Mayor was largely ceremonial. There were five Town Council seats. After the election, the Council itself would vote for one of their own to be the Mayor. Historically, that meant the Mayor ran the Town Council meetings and went to ribbon cuttings and other ceremonies. Even with the title of Mayor, she held no more power than any of the other Town Council members. Joanna Moody was finishing the end of her second term as Mayor and third term on the Council. With her consistent presence, however and the election of a couple of less ambitious but agreeable Council members she had become the de facto leader by seniority, if not leadership ability.

Jillian Dupree had gained tremendous power during her tenure and needed Moody's re-election to give her a buffer against some town folk who had begun to question her acquisition of power. In most towns and cities, the Town Manager worked for and at the pleasure of the Council. Not in Genna, here Jillian Dupree ran the show. She offered up the only data and propositions that the Council would vote on. She controlled what the Council members said to the public. She had her finger on everything that went on. She was not about to let the sewer failure change that. She needed Mayor Moody, simply because she wasn't smart enough to think for herself. That was fine with Jillian, she was smart enough to think for the both of them.

"By the way, Sam Martinez is going to be here in about an hour, he wants to talk to us about that geological assay. He says he has a plan." She said nodding to the file Moody had tossed so haphazardly onto her tidy workspace.

A short time later, Sam arrived and Jillian greeted him out in her office's reception area, then led him to the conference room. *Always Lead* was her motto, but she also used her narrow backside wedged into a knee-length pencil skirt to her advantage as men followed her, she knew she had their attention before the first words were spoken. The Mayor, a homely sort with unkempt stringy brownish-gray hair, was trying to wipe some odd bit of food off her blouse when they walked in. Jillian smirked as the Mayor clumsily stood to shake hands.

"Good to see you, Sam. I need some good news.", She said.

Sam Martinez was a shade under five foot nine with dark brown hair and tan skin; a shade lighter than the dark black hair and deeper skin pigmentation of the rest of his family. His father still suspected that Sam wasn't actually his son, but had never taken it out him. No, that suspicion and the anger behind it had been reserved for his mother for the last forty-five years. Despite the fact that he knew embarrassingly little Spanish, he still had a slight Hispanic accent or inflection on certain words. This was likely due to his upbringing on the outskirts of the Pascua Yaqui Reservation in South Tucson. He had come a long way from living in utter poverty on 'The Rez' to brokering multi-million dollar deals. But that experience growing up had also given him an edge to his demeanor that people often confused with toughness. He preferred to view it more as the drive to get 'it' done, whatever 'it' was.

Sam was something of a fixer. Joanna had met him during her years building highways throughout the State. Whenever they ran into a hurdle; geological impediments, residents fighting easements, funding shortages, whatever they ran into Sam would find a solution and get the project back on track. She had introduced Sam to Jillian when they needed a strong push to get a bond measure passed to cover government pensions, against heavy resistance from the citizens of Genna. After the first two geological surveys failed to deliver a realistic path to a sewer system, she reached out to Sam to help with this last gasp attempt.

"Well, ladies. I think I have a solution." He announced as he pulled his own copy of the latest survey and a large map of the area and spread the map out on the conference table. "The way I see it, you have three primary issues. First, at a little over 24,000 residents, Genna is the largest town in the State of Idaho without a sewer system and the town simply cannot attract manufacturers or larger revenue-generating businesses to the area because the septic tanks simply aren't sustainable for them. Second, with all the surveys that have been done, there simply is no way to build along the western rim because of both the geology and the geography." He pointed at the map, running his finger along the canyon west of town. "We could overcome one or the other, but with both geological and topographical challenges, it is doomed. And, of course, lastly... you have no idea how to pay for it. Fifteen Million dollars? I mean, you guys blew your budget up just to pay for the Environmental Impact studies and Geo Assays."

He paused to look at their defeated faces before spinning the map around so the other side of the town was facing them. "We have never really considered the eastern ridge, primarily because it is further away from what you consider your business corridor and there is no flat easy spot down the canyon to install a treatment plant. But I showed the results from the core samples of this ridge to my people and they became interested." He pointed to his printout which had several mineral values circled: copper pyrites, zinc blende, galena, and tetradymite.

"These don't mean anything is there, but the high concentrations of a few of these minerals could be markers indicating the presence of more valuable minerals underneath this shelf. Valuable enough that they came up with a solution to your problems. They are proposing that they shear off the edge of this ridge to a ninety-degree angle so that they can bolt your sewer right to the cliff face and run it down to here."

He pointed to a tree-covered spot at the base of the canyon. "I have already spoken to the Forestry Department and Bureau of Land Management and have assurance from both that we can obtain this piece of land for the treatment plant right here."

Sam certainly had their attention now. Now to close the deal. He took a deep breath and exhaled long slow and evenly. "They will build your sewer and fund it for you. They want to help bring your beautiful little town into at least the 20th century, if not the 21st. And they want to start right away."

Mayor Moody had the first tears streaming down her face. "Jillian, we're really going to get this done!" she exclaimed. "Finally!"

Jillian Dupree almost cracked a smile on her narrow hawkish face, before regaining her composure. "I like it, Sam. But who are 'they' and what do they want? Nobody is handing out fifteen million dollars without expecting a return on their investment."

Sam feigned offense, "Philanthropists give back to their communities all the time. But I hear you. These guys are venture capitalists that understand that sitting on a mineral claim is a great long-term investment holding. Shaving the edge of that canyon wall to build your sewer pipeline will also let them drill horizontal samples under that shelf to see if the indicators are accurate and determine what minerals might be there."

"They want to mine, Genna?" Jillian chirped louder than she meant to, but she was incredulous.

Sam took a step back and put his hands out in front of him defensively, "No, No, No, they don't want to mine Genna. You can't just mine a town, come on. But owning the mineral rights gives solidity to their investment portfolio, strengthening their positioning on their next big business deal. These guys do multi-billion dollar deals all around the world. Frankly, the fifteen million dollars here is small beans to them, but it is a game-changer for your town. It's a true win-win."

"Okay, that makes sense, I guess. What are the conditions of this deal?"

"They are only really asking for three things in exchange for this." He looked at Joana Moody, "First, you must win the upcoming election. The two of you must retain your leadership roles. These guys don't like uncertainty and changing leadership in the middle of a project could prove disastrous. To that end, they will buy some TV time for you and get you some marketing money. Your challengers are all low dollar small-town handshake campaigners. We'll help you kill them with exposure." He glanced up at Joanna who, in his mind, was not a TV-friendly face and made a mental note to have the guys work up some great messaging for her.

"Second, and this will require some work on your part. There just over thirteen thousand homes in Genna." He pointed to an area along the eastern rim circled in red, "these forty-nine houses will need to be demolished to create the cliff wall for your sewer pipe. That is just zero-point-three percent of the town's homes. I don't care how you do it, but you must acquire these properties. Buy them out, use eminent domain laws to take them. Whatever it takes, and it must be done quickly. Nothing happens until those are acquired."

"But Sam, some of these people aren't going to want to move at any price." The Mayor offered.

"Then you don't get a sewer. It's quite simple." Sam grabbed the map and test results and put them back in his briefcase. "You have three weeks to get yourself re-elected. I'll have the production people come out here tomorrow to get started on a few TV spots. Jillian, that gives you three weeks to figure out how to acquire those properties. I will draw up the paperwork and bring it by at, say nine a.m. tomorrow?"

"The Town Attorney, Owen, will have to sit in on that, just so you know."

Sam nodded, shook hands with both of them and turned on his heel for the door.

"Sam," Jillian called after him. "you said there were three things that they were asking for: For Joanna to win, to acquire the properties and what was third?"

"Oh my, I thought that was clear... We get the mineral rights to those 49 properties."

Chapter Two

Tuesday 8 pm

It was time. He wished it wasn't. He was a good public speaker, so it wasn't that. And this was far from a hostile crowd; he'd handpicked most of the attendees. Tonight, of all nights, he needed to project enthusiasm and optimism, but deep in his gut, he sensed a darkness coming.

He slid his chair back and stood up from the table, which stretched the length of the room. His trademark blue plaid, button-down shirt and black cargo shorts belied the importance of the occasion. He looked down the long table, past the 38 people sipping cocktails and chatting amiably, and caught her eye; nodding toward the center on the far side of the table, as he walked around to meet her there.

There was nobody else in the restaurant, this was a private affair. This particular restaurant was quite new in town and had quickly gained a reputation for flavor and for the classy vibe that emanated from its modern take on 'Old Barn' Chic. They also only served breakfast and lunch, which made it the perfect place to hold tonight's dinner.

"Ladies & gentleman, yes, it's that time. But first, let's give some love to our chef and hosts for opening up just for us tonight." James, lifted his water glass toward the chef, as the crowd cheered and raised their own imbibements toward Tony, which he accepted with a bow.

"Now, I want to thank all of you, not just for coming tonight, but for supporting, helping and sharing our message throughout the campaign. This was a pretty intense campaign at times, especially for this small of a town, and I have to admit that I kinda enjoyed that," he laughed and the crowd followed suit.

"Though, I also have to admit that I am really glad it's over. Tonight, or tomorrow when the results are in, we'll know the outcome. We have done all that we can do. As we planned this event tonight Chrystal and I called this, euphemistically of course, the 'Thank God it's Over Dinner'." He turned and laughed with Chrystal.

"I want you all to know, that win or lose, I am really proud of the campaign we ran. I am really proud that so many people got involved and stood behind our message. I am really glad that we fought hard when we needed to and rallied and unified the townspeople in a way that the folks in town hall never imagined, and I expect that voter turnout today broke records. I'm not going to predict victory. No, it is always difficult to beat an incumbent. I am hopeful, but…" He paused to look around the room, "But I know without a doubt that this little lady, right here, a woman that most of you had never even heard of until three months ago, got enough votes to ensure that Scott Hill doesn't win, that son of a bitch. If you ask me, that alone is worth all the hard work."

"I appreciate the trust you all have put in me and my judgment. But enough about me, let's hear from the woman of the hour, my friend, Chrystal Van Der Linden." James announced as they embraced in a big hug. Then he stepped back and walked away.

This is her show now, he thought to himself. *I am done.*

Wednesday 7 am

He backed out of the driveway of his charming little two-story home and noticed the way that the American flag on the barn-red front deck swayed with the breeze as he shifted into drive and pulled away. The salmon-colored sunrise cast a soft hue over the town. James was on his way to meet some of 'the boys' for coffee and pontificating down on Easy Street. Somehow it kept him centered.

He felt good. Relaxed, for the first time in months, he was eager to move on and figure out what was next. He had been approached a year or so ago about running for Genna Town Council, himself. The current town 'leadership' had no idea how to attract businesses or grow an economy. They were much better at letting the same cronies watch over the slow and steady decline of the beautiful and once prosperous town.

Born James Aloysius Augustine, his parents were distant relatives and great fans of the Irish writer James Augustine Aloysius Joyce, he thought he had a pretty good shot at beating the incumbent. He had only lived in Genna for three years, but had developed a strong voice within the community and knew he could appeal to the masses. Genna had truly become his home and he loved and had become a part this community more than he had anywhere else he had ever lived.

He turned down the invitation anyway. His life had some uncertainty and having to move was a distinct possibility. He wasn't sure that he could commit to a four-year term. If he was honest with himself, he also knew that he had enough skeletons in his closet to turn his endeared following into a lynch mob should they ever come to light. No, it was better for him to work in the background. James wasn't a bad guy, but he had done some bad and stupid things. He had remade himself into an upstanding citizen when he arrived in Genna. Though he never forgot where he came from. In fact, that was why he was heading to Easy Street at seven a.m. on a Wednesday morning to have coffee and conversation with 'the boys' at a meeting of Alcoholics Anonymous.

James checked his phone, knowing that soon messages would start pouring in. A friend at the County Recorder's office had sent him the unofficial election results last night during the dinner, Chrystal hadn't won, but James didn't want to spoil the evening for everyone, so he had kept it to himself. He smiled and allowed himself a quick moment of basking in personal accomplishment. James had taken a largely unknown newcomer to town from obscurity into the limelight. Her own positive energy, unstoppable volunteerism, and southern belle personality had turned the limelight into a genuine cultural movement. He had truly hoped that Chrystal would win, however that wasn't his only objective. He had accomplished his primary goal, extraordinarily well. His secondary goal, well, he had sacrificed that to achieve the primary goal, pulling enough votes from Scott Hill to make sure that he was nowhere near Town Hall.

Genna itself is a beautiful town of just under 25,000 residents, nestled on a ridge just south of Mount Heyburn in west-central Idaho, overlooking the South Fork Salmon River Valley. Near the edge of the Sawtooth National Forest, the area was rich with lakes, rivers, wildlife and covered with Spruce, Fir, Cedar and Pine trees. It was a mountain town at heart, but it had grown to a point that 'city' problems had begun to plague it. Economic growth had ceased two decades before and the slow slide to economic decay had picked up its pace. Much of that lack of progress lay at the feet of the current Town leadership and their lack of vision, in James' opinion. The good ol' boys network at the Genna Chamber of Commerce had continually filled town council spots with a majority of their own adherents. In effect, the same handful of people had run the town for a generation. They had pushed back strongly against new ideas for economic prosperity. Only one of the five current Town Council members, Joshua Florini, had been able to gain enough momentum to gain a seat from outside the circle of power. Of course, any contentious vote ended 4-1 against Joshua. It had been James' hope that he could give Joshua some help and the people of Genna another voice. But alas, it was not to be.

James stopped to grab a dozen donuts to take to the morning meeting, he chatted amiably with the counter clerk, stopped and shook hands with Dave Jones at one of the tables. Dave's wife was the stylist that cut James' hair... If you can call it a style when you've had the same haircut for twenty-five years. In that time, it had morphed from brown to gray to where it was now, more white than anything else. He grabbed his dozen and reached for the door, which opened at that very instant and in walked Scott Hill.

James smirked and kept moving through the door, "Mornin' Scott", he added as he walked to his car. He heard the bell on the donut shop's door clank behind him, he laughed and shook his head, knowing he wasn't going to get to his meeting on time. He carefully placed the donuts on top of his car and turned around as Hill was approaching quickly from behind.

"You son of a bitch. You should be lynched and run outta town for what you did." Scott was practically foaming at the mouth. By now James knew how to push his buttons, and while he wasn't looking forward to any altercation that might alter his good mood, he couldn't help but keep poking.

James, calmly and dripping with sarcasm replied, "Why Scott, whatever do you mean?"

"You singlehandedly put that wretched woman back into the Mayor's office. How could you do that? You know how sickly this town has become in the last seven years. I just can't believe you sided with her."

By now Scott was inches from James' face. James had had enough; he rammed the heels of his palms into Hill's chest and shoved him away. "Get out of my face." He growled as Scott stumbled backward in the gravel. "You know damn well that I didn't choose her. What are you, a five-year-old trying to throw a tantrum? I despise Joana." He took a deep breath trying to ensure he didn't lose control and knock Scott out. James hadn't been in a fight since he got sober, he had been in many before that, but he wanted to keep that record intact. But Scott Hill was the one guy in this town that he might make an exception for.

He rubbed his hand through his hair and turned back towards his car. "But you were the more dangerous asshole in this election. I will start dealing with her now. But I have to admit that though we didn't win either, I have been smiling since I woke." He grabbed the donuts off the roof, noticing that the wind had flipped the box's lip open and climbed into the seat. "Because your narcissistic ass is nowhere near Town Hall. My mission is accomplished. So, fuck you and have a nice day!" He smiled and winked at Hill, as he yanked the door closed and drove away.

He spent the next hour at his meeting trying to be of service to his fellows by sharing his experience, strength, and hope... and his vulnerabilities. At this point in his sobriety, it really wasn't about not drinking anymore, it would take a major life event and a collapse in his spiritual condition to cause him to go out and drink again. But he had seen that happen to others. No, at this point his recovery was about being a better man than he was yesterday. It was about centering himself and living life in the moment and on a more spiritual plane. It was about bringing positivity into negative space. He wasn't religious by any definition, but he had learned to become spiritual through the program. That had been a difficult road for him at the beginning. He had no belief in God and a jaded experience with religion so he had found adopting this fundamental part of AA quite challenging. After all, James' father was Catholic but his mother was Mormon, so he grew up, basically, confused. As life had gone through its peaks and valleys, he'd never really called on nor expected, God's help. Of course, he also hadn't noticed or found gratitude when it was obvious that something greater had interceded on his behalf. Over the course of his sobriety that openness and presence in the moment helped him appreciate and find gratitude for the small things in life.

One mentor, Reverend Dave, had once been speaking at a meeting and had put the difference in perspective that worked for James. He'd said, "Religion is for folks that don't want to go to Hell... Spirituality is for those that have already been there." James could definitely relate to that. He'd been through hell; it had nearly killed him. He wasn't going back.

When he walked out of the meeting room, he saw another kind of hell waiting for him. He took a deep breath of air and walked towards his car.

Leaning against the trunk was the Town Manager Dupree, though not unattractive, she was anorexically skinny and looked likely to blow away as the winds caused her skirt to flap audibly.

"Jillian," he greeted her, "so much for anonymity, huh?"

"It's a small town, James. And you didn't answer my call." He had felt his phone vibrate in his pocket during the meeting, but hadn't yet checked it or turned the ringer back on.

"Let me guess, you're here to thank me for getting Joanna re-elected? No need, I already ran into Scott and he congratulated me for that too, this morning."

She almost laughed, "I bet he did. You really did do the town a service by targeting that jackass. But no, 'WE' got Joana re-elected thank you, you simply made it more interesting."

He searched her eyes trying to figure her intent here. In all these years he had always had to seek her out at her office, on her turf where she had control of the situation. He had only once ever even seen her out at a restaurant. For her to seek him out, as opposed to summoning him, it wasn't normal. "What are you doing here, Jillian? Gloating? What do you want?"

"I want to offer a truce of sorts. Now that the

election is over, maybe we can work together. We both want the same thing, James. Why are we fighting?"

James was flabbergasted, "Clarify the 'we both want the same thing' line before I respond. What does that mean?" He crossed his arms and waited for her response, a sure sign to her that he was closed off emotionally to this conversation, and he knew she would pick up on it. She was smart, there was no question about that. Far more intelligent than Mayor Moody. But she would also cut you off at the knees if you crossed her. It was often difficult, even for James, to get a read on her motives.

"Genna, James, we both want what's best for Genna. I have the power and the will to get things done. You have, at least, proven that you have the people behind you. You're a natural leader and I do believe that your heart is in the right place, but there are realities in government that are difficult to understand from the outside. If you start working with us, rather than against us I think we can accomplish a great deal."

James smirked, "First of all, I've seen your financials and you can't afford me. Second, if I have to hear one more discussion about the damn sewer, I'm going to puke. You cannot justify that kind of price tag on the hopes that maybe, by an act of God, the economy might improve because of it. If you don't have a plan to grow the economy and become a business-friendly environment the sewer won't make a damn bit of difference."

"James, I am not offering you a job, I am offering a chance for us to pool our strengths and work together. As for the sewer, after today, we won't have to discuss that. Between you and me, it's done. I got it funded and construction starts in the next two weeks. I didn't want to announce it during the election because you would have scrutinized the plan and torn Joana's campaign apart. I needed her to win." She swiped a strand of hair, that had stuck to her lipstick, away and walked toward her black Mercedes, "Think about it, huh?"

She left James dumbfounded. On the one hand, this was very interesting. To be a part of the inner circle and help Genna's citizens have a real voice, a real advocate. On the other hand, he didn't trust things that didn't fit. None of that conversation explained why she had sought him out here, instead of simply asking him to stop by Town Hall, unless it was simply to prove she had dirt on him. The conversation also left him with one giant question: *what was in the sewer deal that would have let me tear Joana's campaign apart?*

His iPhone vibrated in his pocket, he opened it to read the text message, assuming that it was the nagging reminder from the iPhone that he'd missed Jillian's call.

"This Is Idaho Electric Power with an important safety and preparedness warning:

Be advised that due to high winds throughout the day Idaho Electric Power may shut off power in your area during the evening and overnight hours if windspeeds increase significantly.

Be prepared for between 8 and 36hrs without electricity.

We apologize for the inconvenience. We at Idaho Electric Power rank Safety as our #1 Priority."

Wednesday 8:30am - Genna Town Hall

Jillian whipped through the covered drive and parked in the reserved spot closest to the south door of the boxy brown building that served as Genna's Town Hall. Quickly, her black heels clicked their way down the rough-cut wooden floors of the hallway towards her office. Just as she set her bag down on the desk, Mayor Moody walked in.

"Thank God, you're here, Jillian. Sam called three times already. He's on his way here."

"I suppose congratulations are in order, Councilwoman Moody." She replied condescendingly. "What does Sam want so urgently?"

"He didn't say, only that he needs to see us both.

I assume it has to do with the election."

Jillian sighed, "Well, at least you won. That should satisfy him for the time being." She stated as she logged into her computer. Her assistant had already placed today's printed schedule on the blotter atop her mahogany desk.

"Not quite satisfied, I am afraid." came Sam's voice from the outer office. As he entered, followed by a tall well-dressed man unknown to either of Jillian or the Mayor.

"Not satisfied, why? She won the election. Everything is going exactly as we had agreed!" Exclaimed Jillian.

She noticed Sam take a slight step to shift to his right, as the other man stepped forward. "You were charged to ensure that you both kept your leadership positions." He said in a quiet, but deeply intense tone.

"Excuse me, who are you, exactly?" Jillian pushed back with a similar intensity.

Sam spoke up, "Jillian Dupree, Councilwoman Moody this is one of my benefactors Gavin David." Though he pronounced it Dah-veed with a flair.

Jillian glanced down at the man's shoes to get a read on him. Her eyebrows raised at the sight of a flawless pair of Berluti Scritti calf leather slip-ons. At more than two thousand dollars a pair, they spoke to a level of wealth rarely, if ever, seen in Genna before. She swallowed. "A pleasure to meet you, Mr. David. What exactly is your complaint? She has won. Our positions are secure. She is the Mayor; I am under contract for two more years."

Gavin laughed, but his eyes were not smiling. "Secure? Are you kidding me? She is NOT the Mayor, she won a Town Council seat. She beat someone that nobody had ever heard of until three months ago by a lousy two hundred votes. An incumbent running for a fourth term should have beaten her by five thousand votes. Hell, if that idiot Scott Hill hadn't run, this Van Der Linden woman would likely have beat you by a landslide." He looked directly into Joanna Moody's eyes. "You have put all of us in jeopardy."

Joanna was clearly out of her depth here and continuously glanced at Jillian waiting for her to jump in. She didn't have to wait long. Jillian was shrewd enough to know the importance of this moment. She shot back sternly, "But SHE WON!! I control the votes on the council and we have enough to get her reappointed to that position next month at the December Council meeting."

"My partners do not share your confidence. If she had won by a wide margin, we could assume that the vote would happen as you prescribe, however with such a weak showing in the election there is too much uncertainty. Florini will oppose her, his popularity with the people makes it a distinct possibility that he can recruit another vote to his side. And if there is no Mayor Moody, there is no buffer to protect you." Gavin took a deep breath before adopting a more conciliatory tone, "But we have already invested millions in this project, so we will have to make due. What is the status of the property and mineral rights of the forty-nine?"

Jillian pulled out a spreadsheet and glanced at it briefly, though she knew the numbers off the top of her head. She also knew that they would not please this man any more than the election results had. She had delegated the acquisition of properties to her Assistant Town Manager, Marcus. He was an ambitious man, but the push-back from residents had been more significant than either of them had expected. She noticed a slight tremor in the hand holding the paper and quickly dropped it back on the desk.

"We have acquired thirteen outright, two are in foreclosure, but we will get those shortly. Three are either abandoned or have been unoccupied for several years. If we can find the owners, we should be able to get those easily enough. The rest are in negotiation." Jillian answered. She glanced at Sam hoping that their relationship would gain her an ally, but he had clearly taken a backseat to Gavin David showing no sign of wanting to wade into these waters.

"So, eighteen?" Mr. David snarled. "That's if we count the maybes... so really thirteen? Fifteen, if I assume you are capable of gaining the two foreclosures." He began pacing back and forth across the office. When he came to a stop, he appeared resolute. "Since you two have let us down on two fronts there is only one way to proceed. Have your clerk sign all of the permits for the project for me to take with me today. We must move up the time-line." He strode purposefully out the door.

Sam followed along as Gavin David pulled out his cell phone hit one number and put it to his ear. He spoke quietly, "You have the list of forty-nine. Thirty-four need to be made compliant, do whatever you need to do, just get it done."

As they walked past the service counter in the hallway, a man reached out and handed him a stack of permits. Gavin grabbed them without slowing or saying a word and continued out the door.

Wednesday 6 pm- Genna, Idaho

Tristan Byrne cracked open a cold beer as he settled into the wicker chair perched on the large deck off the back of his double-wide mobile home. He flicked the cap between his thumb and middle finger towards the open 5-gallon Lowe's bucket which served to collect the empty bottles for recycling, the caps banged off the lip before falling onto the deck near the other three that had also missed. The wind had ramped up as the day had progressed, right now the gusts sounded like waves crashing on a reef, though he was over seven hundred miles from the nearest seashore.

He stared up towards the sky, surveying the tall pines that surrounded his yard, looking for dead or broken branches. Tristan had just returned home after his shift. As the wind had steadily increased today, they'd gone on four 'widow-maker' calls this afternoon alone. Tristan had been a firefighter for ten years now, but until he moved up to Genna he had never even heard of a widow-maker. Apparently, the long dry summer season combined with a late start to the rainy season caused dead or broken branches to become brittle. In winds like these, branches from fifty or sixty feet up the tree could shear off, falling toward the ground like a silent missile. If a person happens to be outside and in the path between the branch and the ground, they would likely never know what hit them as they were impaled, thus making their wives into widows... Widow-maker. The calls that they had been on today hadn't been fatal, luckily, but it certainly gave you a sense of respect how dangerous this beautiful forest they lived in could be.

His phone dinged from across the patio,

indicating a text had come in. *I'll get it when I get up.* He thought to himself, taking another sip of his Corona.

He laid his head back and closed his eyes, listening to the wind. He exhaled a long breath as he relaxed for the first time all day. Wind causes all kinds of problems and made for an extremely hectic day as limbs fall and trees crack and fall onto roads and structures, causing accidents and injuries. They had been lucky today, none of the wind-related calls had been terribly severe. Of course, all of these calls were on top of the normal daily calls involving shop injuries, heart attacks, car accidents and such. But everyone had lived, it was a good day.

Tristan jerked awake with a start. He hadn't meant to doze off. He had no idea what time it was nor how long he had slept, but the sun was long gone and the wind had picked up considerably. He searched his pockets for his phone to check the time, before remembering that it was across the patio on the railing plugged into a charger.

As he stood, something flapping from the edge of his roof caught his eye. He took a few steps closer and saw that it was a large clump of pine needles still attached to a twig. He looked closer and noticed how full his gutters were. *I need to spend some time this weekend cleaning these gutters.*

The irony wasn't lost on him that he actually

coached residents about fire prevention efforts; keeping gutters clear and creating a hundred feet of defensible space around their house that was free of debris. Living in a forest these were major concerns, but his focus now was on having the gutters cleared for drainage once the first snows come.

He put his thumb on the biometric reader on his phone to open it up. It was now showing four new messages: One each from Idaho Electric, Bear County, Town of Genna and from his fire department. All of them saying the exact same thing:

"This Is Idaho Electric with an important safety and preparedness warning:

Be advised that due to high winds throughout the day Idaho Electric may shut off

Power in your area during the evening and overnight hours if windspeeds increase significantly.

Be prepared for between 8 and 36hrs without electricity.

We apologize for the inconvenience. We at Idaho Electric rank Safety as our #1 Priority."

Well, at least they are giving people a heads up. Being a first responder, he liked the high-tech notification systems now, even if they were a bit redundant, they helped people get prepared. It might also make tomorrow's shift less chaotic. Before he went in to retire for the night, he went out to his shed to ensure his backup generator had fuel. It's always good to be prepared.

<u>Chapter Three</u>

Thursday 6:27 am – Rome, Idaho

Michael had just arrived at his office, twelve miles down the hill from Genna, in the City of Rome. He was a marketing consultant, temporarily on contract to a mid-size nutraceutical company. At 50, he was trying to figure out where he fit in the business world today. In truth, he was over-qualified for most jobs in small rural towns, but that was where his heart was drawn. That was where he and his wife had chosen to raise their seven-year-old son, Stuart. Though they lived in Genna, his son went to a Montessori school in Rome and Michael had put his office here since there was a larger business community than in Genna. His phone was sitting on the window sill, that his desk fronted when it dinged. He preferred that his desk face the window that looked out at the orchards that spread along this portion of the valley. He glanced at his phone, the notification was from a Facebook group he subscribed to called Bear County WIX Spotter which reported on traffic, accidents, fires, and crimes. He opened the link, it said:

"6:27am Reporting party describes Spot Fire as 50 ft by 50 ft located near Bonneville Rd and Lewis Ranch. 22 miles SE of Genna. 17 miles E of Rome -Source/cause Unknown
Units are en route"

Michael knew Bonneville Rd well; it was the route up to Bear Canyon Lake. There were fires along there frequently, usually from the chains on someone's boat trailer dragging on the asphalt and sending sparks flying into the dry grass along the roadside. There was little else out there. Even Lewis Ranch was over five thousand acres with the houses and structures all on the far side of the property, well away from the fire. He wasn't the type to overreact to these things, there had been fires during the summer that had come much closer, yet had been stopped in the canyons. But there was something in the pit of his gut that he couldn't shake. With this wind, who knew? He quickly shared the post onto the local Rants & Raves page which had more than sixteen thousand members, so that those who were up this early could at least have warning and follow the developments if there were any.

Michael then dialed his wife, who would be getting ready to take their son down to school in Rome. "Hi, don't freak out." He paused and chastised himself, that kind of opening line ensured that whoever was on the other end would freak out.

"There is a small fire down by Bonneville and something feels wrong to me. It may be nothing. But do me a favor and call your mother. I want you to wake her up and tell her to grab a bag of clothes and go to John's."

Her recently widowed mother had a new boyfriend who lived two towns over, well the other direction from the fire.

"But why, if you think this is nothing?"

"Because, if this goes bad, I won't have to deal with two households, just ours. Please just do it, it will make me feel better. I will keep an eye on it. Just call me once you drop Stuart off at school and hopefully, I will have some more information."

Thursday 6:42 am -Genna Ridge Hospital

The hospital was prepared for the brief power shut off that occurs between the time that power is cut to the facility and the time it takes for the backup generators to come online. That never happened. Eric had been working the night shift and they had been ready for the transition as they had been warned by Idaho Electric Power, but the power had held steady all night. As the sunrise heralded the end of his shift, Eric went down to sign out and noticed a group of nurses gathered around the Charge Nurse's desktop computer. They were fairly animated, he assumed that it was some marginally inappropriate video. He had learned to deal, in this environment, with the same behavior that women dealt with in every other workplace. He was woefully outnumbered, but he enjoyed the banter.

"How big is it?" one of the nurses asked as she joined the group. Perhaps it wasn't as 'marginally' appropriate as he had originally thought.

He laughed and asked, "What in the world are you ladies watching?"

"There's a fire down by Bonneville Rd." came the reply. Eric stopped laughing.

Bonneville? That's two ridges over, certainly of no concern to us. He thought. But the talk was urgent. It always was when there was a fire in the area, the hospital had been shut down before due to a fire in the canyon. The hospital facilities were situated off of Pulga Rd, right along the edge of the canyon on the east side of Genna.

"How big is it?"

"It just updated; it was fifty-foot by fifty-foot maybe five minutes ago. Firefighters have just arrived on scene and it's now estimated at two hundred acres." Nurse Gina replied, with a worried look on her face.

"It's still awfully far away, we shouldn't be impacted, but it would be good for someone to keep an eye on it," Eric said, trying to alleviate any fears. He finished signing out, before walking down the hallway and out the glass front doors into the parking lot. He looked to the left and could see a plume of smoke. Bonneville Rd was quite a distance away, but the smoke seemed closer than that somehow. Colored the dark black and purple of fire with plenty of fuel. Eric knew it did too. The unusually wet spring gave rise to plenty of wild grass and vegetation. But it was followed by a very dry summer and a nearly nonexistent fall rainy season. Combine all of that with the oxygen in these winds, yeah, that sounds like a bad combination. But again, it was two ridges away and he had faith that the firefighters could handle it. He took a deep breath of fresh air. It didn't smell like smoke, and he was downwind of the fire. He turned on his heel and headed back in to finish updating a couple of patient charts before he went home.

Thursday 6:44 am -Bonneville Rd

Fire Captain Kori Davies pulled up to an unexpected scene at the 'Origin'. Though the sun was just rising, it was midnight dark here. The small spot-fire had been called in seventeen minutes ago. His first crews had arrived on the scene nine minutes ago. He had expected to be seeing the mop up when he got here, but they had made next to no progress. The fire was raging and covered more than a square mile, over six hundred and forty acres, by his estimate. He glanced up the hill to get an idea of the distance to the next structure. The wind was calmer this morning that it had been late yesterday, but it was still blowing. He walked up to the nearest of his men.

"What's the situation, Johnny? As bad as it looks?"

"Worse, Cap. This is a shit show. The terrain here won't let us get near it. We can't even get to the front edge without a chopper, the grass is knee-high and dead covering rocks and crevasses. I'm not getting my guys stuck out there. We need to get a bunch of crews up there on Hwy 52," he pointed to the nearest ridge, "maybe if we can get a handle on that line, we might be able to stop it there. But they better get there quick, this thing is moving fast. If it gets to that tree line... well, I don't even want to think about it."

As he finished speaking, the sun crested the mountains to the east. The added energy could be felt almost instantly. The fire flared up as the wind gusted. The roaring blaze nearly doubled in size in under a minute as it became apparent that it wasn't just a gust.

The wind had arrived.

Captain Davies got on his radio. "Dispatch, we need to get a break set up on Hwy 52, get all available units in surrounding counties headed this way." He gazed across the hellish field, "And pray we don't need them."

Thursday 6:58 am -Rome, Idaho

Sheriff Ezra Horne, freshly showered and shaved, walked into the kitchen to make breakfast. It was unusual for him to be this late, his internal body clock usually had him up at 5:15, it was like clockwork with his system. No need for alarms, he awoke within two minutes one way or the other of that time every day and had for years. But not today, it was strange. Though winter was approaching, the days hadn't shortened that significantly, yet it seemed darker than usual. He followed his normal routine; two eggs over-easy and a bowl of mixed fruit.

Ezra was a man of habit, and his routines worked for him. At six-foot-two and two hundred twenty-five pounds, he cut an imposing figure that belied his fifty-four years. He was something of a local legend as a leader, especially since the Bear County Reservoir's dam had nearly failed last year and the way he had handled the evacuation of the areas below the dam. He didn't necessarily like the 'Legend' status that came with that. He was simply doing his job to the best of his abilities. One of his deputies had even shown him some memes on

Facebook that praised him in over the top ways, even comparing him to the toughness of Chuck Norris, the movie star. He was moved but embarrassed by that kind of thing.

When he was finished eating, he rinsed his plate and as he bent down to stack it into the dishwasher, he caught a glimpse out the window in the front room. The coloring was all off, the lawn, trees and even the air seemed to have a rust-colored tinge to it. He glanced behind him out the kitchen window to the west and it was normal dawn colors and blue skies. He immediately reached down to his waist and turned on his radio. The radio chatter shattered his peaceful, relaxing morning as he rushed to gather his things and hustle to his patrol car. Ash was slowly falling onto his windshield like an early snow.

Thursday 7:15 am – Hwy 52 along Carbon Gap

Engine 69 and her crew were the first to arrive at the top of the ridge to create a break for the fire. The men jumped out to assess the situation and make a plan to fight it. Tristan reached the edge and looked down into the valley. The smoke was thick, dark and heavy. He could see the swath the fire had cut in, he glanced at his watch, forty-eight minutes. The fire was running like an arrow formation; narrow at the origin, ever wider as it moved across the grasslands and now as it hit the base of the rocky ridge that he was standing on it appeared to be spreading its arms out wide, running four or five miles each direction from where he was. He looked back at the guys, they were masked up and hurriedly unloading hoses. A tractor-trailer had arrived, its occupants scrambling to unload the bulldozer from the trailer to widen the firebreak.

Tristan pulled his own mask on over his head and hustled over to help with the hoses. Halfway there an enormous gust threw Tristan against the side of the fire engine, knocking his helmet off. Behind the truck, the hose was flying like a kite string and one of the men was on the ground. The heavy hose nozzle ended up nearly forty feet away. As Tristan stooped down to help his friend up, the air changed. The color of the sky changed. The temperature changed. He turned to look up and against the dark black smoke he saw a swarm of billions of what appeared to be orange fireflies arcing up and over them and the trucks and the road.

"Oh Shit," he started yelling to the guys, "get loaded back up, we need everything back on the truck. Now. Now. Now!"

The fire had gone airborne. He rushed back to the guys with the trailer to tell them to stop unloading, but they were already cranking down the ratchet chains. As he jogged back to his truck, he braved another peek down the canyon and was surprised to see the fire line still nearly a quarter-mile away. How had it jumped them from that far? The raining of hot embers hadn't let up, arcing like some hellish rainbow. He had never seen anything like it. He raced back to the cab and climbed in.

"Chief," he radioed, "This damn thing went airborne before we even got the first hose off the truck. We're gonna need to redirect all incoming up to Genna. We're going to have to fight it from above. Have we got air support, yet?"

"Negative air support. They have no visibility."

"Tell them to drop blind, we're already losing this race, Chief."

"Copy That. Not my call. Head up and rally at Genna Ridge Hospital. We'll fight this thing from the rim with everything we've got."

Tristan slammed his hand on the steering wheel out of frustration before releasing the brakes and putting it in drive.

Thursday 7:18 am – Genna, Idaho

"Fuck," she moaned as the phone vibrated on her nightstand... again!

Hailey had been up most of the night with her fussy two-year-old son, who had been restless for no obvious reason. Thank goodness that none of the

42

commotion had woken the baby. Her husband, John, had tried to help, but Noah needed his momma. Besides John was scheduled early for work. As a matter of fact, he had been getting ready to leave for work when Hailey finally collapsed into bed.

She just knew John was trying to get her up to take the kids to school, "Fuck it, he can get mad all he wants, I'm taking the kids to school late and sleeping in..."

Just the effort that it took to think up and internalize that response woke her just enough that when the phone started vibrating again, she blindly reached for it, nearly knocking the half-empty water glass from the nightstand. As she pulled her hand back the phone slipped from her grasp and plopped onto the carpet under the edge of the bed.

With a sigh, she said, "Screw it!" and dozed back off.

Thursday 7:33 am - Rome, Idaho

Michael had been following the developments from his office. It didn't look good; his gut had been right again. He was glad he had made the early call to evacuate his Mother-in-law. He had turned on the scanner app on his computer so he could hear the emergency frequencies and get a clearer picture of what was going on. It didn't make him feel any better. Just then his phone rang, the caller ID showed his wife's name.

"Hi, are you on the way to bring Stuart to school?"

"Yes, we just got on the road. It's not smoky here, but it sure is dark."

"Did your Mom get packed up and gone?"

"Not yet, I just called her, you need to talk to her."

"Why do I need to talk to her? I called you to get her going over an hour ago."

"I know, I know. She is up, but she was eating breakfast when I just called. You need to call her; she listens to you."

"Crap... OK, I will call her. After you drop Stuart off, I want you to park somewhere close until you hear back from me. This is getting ugly, but I will know more by then. I will call you in a few."

He tried, unsuccessfully, to roll back his frustration level as he dialed his Mother-in-law Janet's landline. Who in this day and age has a landline, anyway? She had a cellular flip phone, but rarely charged it and used it even less. He let it ring hoping she wouldn't answer because she was on the road. On the third ring, she picked up the handset.

Michael let out an audible sigh, "Janet, I had really hoped you weren't still there to answer."

"Oh, I am almost done getting things together."

"I had Christy call you more than an hour ago. I wouldn't have done that if I didn't think it was important. This is not a drill. Grab your purse, get in your car and drive away right now. You do not want to get stuck once the evacuation begins and I am certain that will happen soon. Leave now!"

"Okay, okay."

Janet lived in a fairly high-end, gated retirement community. She pulled out of the garage attached to her newly painted, cream and copper-colored, home and onto the street. Though it was somewhat more 'cookie-cutter' than most areas of this little mountain town, it was really quite well kept. As she drove slowly through the complex, she noticed that nobody's garage doors were open, nobody was walking, nobody was panicking about this. In fact, nobody seemed to even be here. Michael is just being dramatic, she thought. Just then her headlights automatically kicked on and she realized how dark it had become. She glanced at the rear-view, saw the billowing black plume of smoke, and understood, instantly, what Michael had meant when he had said, "…This is not a drill."

Thursday 7:35 am - Pulga Rd, Genna, ID

Sheriff Horne pulled into the town of Genna behind several fire engines, which he was glad to see, but which also slowed the uphill trek to a much slower crawl than he had wanted. He had taken 'the long way' to come up Pulga Rd because it traversed the eastern edge of Genna and he wanted the best vantage point to see the fire's progress with his own eyes before he reached the town and had to start making decisions and take control of the situation on the ground. He was the top law enforcement officer in the county after all.

The drive was surreal. The beauty of crawling the edge of the pine-covered forest ridge, but that beauty was painted on a very black canvas of smoke and destruction. The plume had changed in color and perhaps even density during the last few minutes of his drive up the hill. Despite all the reports from the Fire Captain that the fire was still several miles away, it appeared to Ezra that the blaze was racing him to town.

He was glad to see some downhill traffic, which caused him not to be able to pass the slower fire trucks. Pulga Road was a two-lane secondary route out of the town of Genna. He sincerely hoped the other routes were steady as well, but as he glanced at his watch, he knew that many of the residents of this sleepy mountain retreat were likely asleep and unaware of the approaching danger. He keyed his mic. "Dispatch, Sheriff Horne here. Get every available unit, deputy, flagman, crossing guard and corrections officer headed to Genna to prepare for mass evacuation. I will update in ten."

He followed the fire trucks into the Genna Ridge Hospital complex. He was pleased to see several already there. Fire Captain Davies' Ford Expedition was parked at the far side of the hospital parking lot, about one hundred yards from the edge of the canyon. Ezra pulled up next to him.

"Kori, what's the current situation?"

The Captain took a deep breath to gain his composure before he answered. His job was to be in control of the situation and protect this town. Just then the wind ripped the hat off his head and in less than five seconds, blew it all the way to the hospital where it was held up by wind pressure against the wall... on the second level.

"Well, the only person that I want to be less than you, right now, is me. We're clocking sixty-five mile per hour winds coming up the lip of this ridge right here. The fire hit the tree line two minutes ago. This thing is moving like nothing we have ever seen. The surface fire has, in some parts transitioned into a crown fire. In other areas, the surface fire is keeping pace with the crown fire. Uphill through those trees, it's still spreading at around three football fields per second. Air support has no visibility. With these winds, we can't risk backburning, and truthfully it doesn't work that well going downhill anyway. I just reached out to the NIFC to see who they can scramble, but I'm not optimistic that they can help quickly enough. We're going to make our stand here, but you need to evacuate this town. I don't even know if we can slow it down, much less stop it."

The Sheriff looked over the edge, beneath the smoke, at ground level he could see the flames coming off of the towering pines, as they licked into and preheated the trees above and in front of them, drying them quickly before the flames leaped uphill to the next tree. This was not good. The flames were maybe half a mile away. As he turned back towards the Fire Captain, something flashed in of the periphery of his vision. He turned to look as flying embers carried by the wind landed in one of the two pine trees perched right at the edge of the hospital parking lot. Right next to him, within seconds the tree ignited. Not five seconds later the tree was fully engulfed in flame as the winds fanned the flames. He stepped back as firefighters, who were just finishing preparation to start battling the blaze down the hill, turned their hoses on and blasted the tree.

"Okay, we'll launch the evac... buy us as much time as you can." The two shook hands as only those who have gone into battle together would. "Stay safe."

The Sheriff keyed his mic as he strode towards

the hospital. "Dispatch, Sheriff Horne, launch evacuation notification system. Mandatory for Genna Zone 4. Evac warning for all other zones."

"Copy, mandatory Zone 4, Sheriff." The speaker repeated in his ear.

Ezra knew the emergency plans for the area. He also knew they would fail. The town was divided into thirteen zones. Zone 4 ran along the ridge that he was standing on, up about three miles north of the hospital. He needed those folks on the road now, but he had no manpower at the moment to go door to door. He had maybe an hour to get twenty-five thousand people off this hill with only four evacuation routes. And he was about to shut one of those down.

"Dispatch, find GPD Chief Stanton and tell him I'm at the hospital launching evac procedures. Get the State Police to close Pulga RD from the hospital south, both ways to non-emergency personnel."

"Sheriff?"

"We need to keep it clear while you get every ambulance and school bus in the county up here to evac the hospital and the schools."

The Sheriff jogged toward the main hospital entrance, as he walked through the doors he announced, in his most commanding voice, "Who's in charge here?"

Thursday 7:38 am – Genna, ID

James hopped out of the shower, later than usual. Usually, he was at his morning meeting by now. He was more drained from the long, contentious election than he had realized. He quickly shaved and got himself ready for the day. He pulled on his favorite blue plaid shirt. He had several, it was a running joke amongst his friends that he wore the same shirt every day. The truth was he had, seven different blue plaid shirts. It wasn't intentional, he rarely even realized it when he was shopping. James hated shopping. He used to tell people that he didn't shop, he bought. If he needed a shirt, he would simply walk in and find the right size, of which there was usually a limited selection, and choose the one that he didn't hate. Somehow, he would arrive home and only then realize it was yet another blue plaid pattern.

After dressing, and walking down the stairs James grabbed his phone to call Joshua Florini. Josh was the one Town Council member that he saw eye to eye with on most issues. The relevant exception to this was that Josh had endorsed Scott Hill for the open Council seat during the election. Though the two had talked regularly, even at the dinner for Chrystal on Tuesday night, James just wanted to smooth things over and make sure that they were good. They hadn't spoken since the 'official results' had come out. He pulled up Josh's number and hit call. Nothing happened. He tried again. Nothing happened. Then he noticed the 'No Service' message where his connectivity bars should be.

"Crap."

Living in a mountain town, it was normal to have spotty cell reception and even spottier data service, but it was very uncommon for him to have 'No Service' here at the house. James went over to his laptop and turned it on. As soon as the boot-up process had finished, he logged into Facebook to send Josh a message. But when Facebook opened the first post that he saw was a photo that his friend Amber had posted of the Genna CVS drug store, less than half a mile from his home, with a massive wave of black smoke billowing up behind it.

James didn't wait for confirmation. He didn't look for an evacuation notice, he simply opened a new post and typed, *"Genna, Evacuate Now! This is Not a Drill!!"*, hopeful that if even one person saw it that it might buy them a few extra minutes to get off the hill.

He needed to find out what was going on. He walked over to his 'pocket basket', where he emptied his pockets at the end of the day. He grabbed his keys, wallet, AA medallion, and his nail clippers. He's a guitar player, he always kept his nails trimmed. He also grabbed his concealed carry weapon, a Smith & Wesson 9mm Shield. He didn't carry it every day, but he did carry often. The truth was he had never felt he needed it since he moved to Genna, but he had carried it for so many years that he often felt naked without it. He tucked the holster inside the right-side waistband of his cargo shorts. He took a quick glance around and decided that information was what he needed the most. He would go see what was happening before he came back and decided if the needed to pack up anything before evacuating. He headed for his car.

Thursday 7:45 am - Genna Ridge Hospital

Eric walked down the hallway having just caught up on his patient charts. As he neared the hospital there was a flurry of activity in the hallways as staff tried to get patients stabilized and cued up to be evacuated. Everyone was hurried, but not panicked. These nurses and staff had been through evacuations before, they had also been drilled on it. A door to the right slammed open in front of him, nearly catching him smack in the face, as a nurse and an orderly wheeled a gurney out of the delivery room and towards the recovery room. When the nurse, Danielle, saw the commotion in the hallway she stopped abruptly and looked at Eric.

"What's going on?" Her patient had had an emergency C-section as pre-eclampsia had progressed to the point that both mom and the baby were in distress. The surgery itself was complicated by excessive scar tissue in the abdominal cavity leftover from a decade-old previous surgery for a bowel resection due to a Meckel's pouch rupture. The surgeon decided that the danger of closing her up without cleaning up much of the scar tissue could cause long-term problems. After all, the C-section would create more scar tissue as it healed anyway. What should have been a ten to fifteen-minute procedure, had taken just over an hour. Mom and baby were fine, but the surgical team was out of the loop with what was happening at the hospital.

"There's a fire in the canyon. They are evacuating the patients to Rome General."

"We can't move her, she's just out of surgery."

"So, take her to Recovery, then go check in with the Charge Nurse, or whoever is running the evac and let her know the situation. I've been off for an hour; I am going home to check on things. I'll be back if you guys need me."

Eric slalomed his way through gurneys, wheelchairs, and nurses, as he made his way to the door and out to the staff parking lot. He was glad to see numerous fire engines and tanker trucks along the far side of the parking lot. The hospital was in good hands. When he reached his BMW, Eric saw something sticking out from under the front left wheel. He picked it up and saw that it was a baseball cap with the Fire Department shield on the front. He looked back to see if anyone was looking for it, but they were all facing the canyon; hoses arcing jets of water over the edge. He decided he'd return it later. He opened the door and tossed the hat and his bag onto the passenger seat and climbed in. It was then that he saw the embroidering on the back, *'Captain Davies'*, it read in yellow thread against the red background fabric.

Thursday 7:47am – Genna, ID

Startled by the front door banging open, Hailey jumped and sat up in her bed, disoriented and cloudy. Had she overslept? It was still dark outside; she couldn't have overslept. She heard footsteps racing down the hallway. *Joe is at work. Who the hell was this? Where are the kids?* was her next thought as adrenaline pumped her awake. Joe burst through the bedroom door.

"Hailey, get your ass out of bed. The fire jumped the canyon."

"What fire? What canyon?" Then it dawned on her, "Wait, our canyon?"

They lived at 1771 Breyer Drive, just off of Pulga Road, a few streets up past the hospital, to the north. They lived right on the canyon. Hailey got up to run outside. She can see several spot fires on Breyer burning, including one very tall pine tree that was just beginning to roar. She and her husband both look at each other and launch into action. Joe starts loading the kids up in the car. Hailey is frantically throwing things that they need for the kids into the living room, Joe's grabbing them and loading up the van. She ran to go put some clothes on, she barely noticed the deafening silence in the bathroom as she changed. She would crave that soon. It disappeared as she opened the door and came out of the bathroom to the kids screaming so loud and her husband yelling, "NOW HAILEY, NOW!"

Hailey looked out the front window and could see three of the neighbors' houses on fire. She ran out the door toward the mini-van as her husband jumped into his work truck. She came to a screeching halt, as she remembered, "Fuck! The keys!"

She whipped around thinking, *Omg, they could be anywhere.* Her two-year-old loved playing with those keys, which also meant they were rarely where they were supposed to be. She often had to search for them before leaving the house. As she ran in through the still-open door, she saw them hanging on the hook where they belong.

"Thank you, God. Thank you, Moses." She sprinted to the van and jumped in. She put her foot on the pedal and noticed she hadn't put on shoes or grabbed any; and she had left the door wide open, again.

Now, she could hear the fire, it's so loud. They never talk about the sound of fire, but she knew then that she would never get that sound out of her head. She hit the gas pedal and pulled out of the driveway, giving her house one last look before speeding off.

Thursday 7:48 am – Rome, ID

Michael raced to gather his things and climbed into his car. He needed to get back up to Genna. As he pulled out, he hit the button on his steering wheel to call his wife.

"Hi."

"Hi, where are you?"

"I'm still in the parking lot at Stuart's school. Parked as you asked. Where are you?"

"I am on my way back up the hill, to get the dogs, and see what the situation looks like."

"And the cat." She snapped, then resolved to do it herself. "Ok, I'll meet you there."

"No, stay where you are, please."

The last time they had evacuated due to a fire in the other canyon, he had sent them off to her mother's place on the other side of town while he stayed with the animals at the house, waiting to see how it developed before evacuating the pets and himself. That time they had been lucky, firefighters and planes dropping fire retardant had kept the fire in the canyon. He had never had to leave the house. He didn't envision today working out that well.

"I am closer than you are, I am going home!"

"Damn it, Christy. Please don't. You and Stuart are safely out of town, I feel better knowing that. I will go do what needs to be done. Stay there. Try to connect with your Mom and make sure that she made it down the hill. If they start evacuating, we'll be stuck in traffic for who knows how long, someone needs to be there for Stuart when school gets out."

They said their goodbyes and hung up as Michael reached the overpass that would take him to The Ridgway, the main drag that would take him from Rome into downtown Genna. While he sat at the light waiting to turn and go across the overpass, he looked over and noticed much heavier traffic there than normal. It was normal for there to be traffic here at this time, it was nearly eight o'clock on a Thursday morning after all. But the traffic should all be coming downhill to work, the backup that he was watching was both ways.

Following his gut, Michael turned the other way and sped down the on-ramp for Hwy 95 South. He would head to Genna the back way, past the Bear

County Waste Dump on Deal Rd. The closer he got to the hill, the darker the sky had turned. For the first time, the smoke had begun to settle closer to the ground, too. He unconsciously pressed harder on the accelerator as it became clear this was going to be as bad as he had feared.

He roared down the highway, now only two miles before the turnoff to Deal Rd. Red and blue lights appeared in his rear-view mirror. In the pitch black, the lights were blindingly bright.

"Shit." He muttered as he glanced at the digital 92 on his dashboard speed indicator. He didn't have time for this and was tempted to push through to the turnoff, now less than a mile away. But alas, that simply wasn't who he was. Michael lifted his foot off the accelerator to slow down as he turned on his blinker and slid into the right lane. To his surprise, the Sheriff's deputy blew past him on route to somewhere else.

"Thank God, for small miracles."

He accelerated again and switched lanes, dropping in behind the speeding cruiser. The deputy pulled into the turning lane to turn left onto Deal Road, but instead of speeding up the road, he slid his patrol car in sideways and came to a stop blocking the road.

"No, no, no... No!"

Michael pulled his car up perpendicular to the patrol car and climbed out. He approached the deputy, who was just getting out of his car with a handful of flares in his hand.

"Sir, I need to get up there. I need to get my dogs out of the house."

"Not this way. All roads are now closed going up the Ridge."

"Come on, man. You know you only beat me here because I did the right thing and pulled over for you. Give me a break."

"I appreciate that. But the road is now closed. The Sheriff has ordered a full evacuation. All incoming traffic is prohibited." He walked along behind his patrol car and began lighting and placing the flares to extend the area of his control. Just then a second patrol car arrived, this one an Idaho State Trooper.

Michael cursed himself as he walked back to the car. If only he had acted as soon as his gut told him to, but no, he had stayed in his office gathering information. Now he was too late. All he could do was pray.

Thursday 7:53 am – Genna, ID

Eric left the hospital parking lot heading south

on Pulga Road. He had seen at least three tall pines trees entirely engulfed in flames on the south side of the hospital campus but the firefighters were right on those fires, attacking them instantly. But the sun was still shining, the smoke wasn't that thick, and there were no flames further down Pulga. Houses were still standing. The traffic was sparse. He wasn't particularly concerned. He reached the turnoff to Benson Road. Moments later a police officer would be stationed here directing folks onto Benson, blocking escape down Pulga Rd. But for now, the shot straight down Pulga Road was open. But Eric had to get home. Benson was the way. Down in the Benson Road dip between two small rises the traffic started. Both ways. As much traffic headed into the fire as away from it. He thought about all the people headed towards the fire but had no opinion of it; they were doing what they had to do, a mixture of duty, bravery, and foolishness. The further across town he got the more it became just a line of cars going the other way. What struck him was the politeness of everyone. No honking. People allowed other people to cut in from side streets. When sirens blared everyone cut over to the curb and let the emergency vehicles through. So much stress and so much dignity. He was proud of his townsfolk. No panic. Of course, none of them had been as close as he had. They really didn't understand what they were driving into.

Eric started worrying a bit more when he noticed

that none of the emergency vehicles heading towards the fire were fire trucks. Police cars, sheriff cars, unmarked cars, fire supervisor cars, but he saw no fire trucks, except the four at the hospital. They needed fire trucks. All the police officers in the county weren't going to stop this fire.

By the time he reached Starke Road, a mere two miles from where he started, things were becoming surreal. It was black as night. Everyone had their headlights on. Ash had fallen across the windshield. Still, he figured that he was safe once he crossed Starke Road. Starke was a wide road and many areas, on each side, had sparse trees, commercial buildings and parking lots. Certainly, even in the worst-case scenario, a fire line could be held at Starke. No way the fire could jump that.

As traffic moved slowly and steadily both directions on Benson in front of Anthony's Appliances, Eric wondered if everyone else felt the same, because everyone was still being very polite and composed. No panic. As he got to Black Olive things got lighter. No need for headlights. At Benson and Ridgway everyone was obeying the traffic lights and once Eric turned onto Ridgway traffic was brisk going both ways. He headed south. Still no fire trucks. He arrived home, just a few streets down, and his wife was standing in the driveway along with his daughter. His daughter, who had gone to work in Rome at six a.m. What was she doing there?

Thursday 7:51 am – Genna, ID

James cruised through town in a surreal state of wonder. He had had a couple of unique surreal drives in his life, but they had always happened in the aftermath of something happening.

He had lived in the Hollywood Hills in a guest house, built on stilts on the edge of a gorge right off of Mulholland Drive when the Northridge earthquake had awoken him at four-thirty in the morning by dropping a bookcase on his bed as he slept. The balcony, which also served as the entrance to his guest house crashed down the steep hillside. He had run barefoot and leapt the gap to reach the asphalt driveway to escape his perilously unstable home. In a deep darkness broken only by the blue flashes of exploding electrical transformers, he had decided to get off the hill and go into Hollywood to assess the damage at the recording studio where he worked on Fairfax, just below Santa Monica Boulevard. The drive was amazingly surreal: he drove down Franklin to Hollywood Blvd, then down Sunset to Fairfax. This was normally the heart of Hollywood; always full of people and activity. But It was all dark and empty; no neon signs, no traffic lights, no cars. Not a single other car was on the road. That was the morning he actually learned what the word surreal meant, and felt like. It was a truly unique experience.

James had also lived in New York on 9/11,

where he learned a much less unique and more horrifying definition of the word, surreal while volunteering during those first few days; digging through rubble, ostensibly searching for survivors, but really just collecting body parts.

This was different, he had that same feeling, but nothing had happened yet. On the west side of town, it wasn't even smoky yet. But there was an ominous beauty and peace in the town. The sun had come up, though the smoke diffused light in different shades and different angles, giving a totally different look to places he drove past every day. In some areas it was black as night; in others, it seemed more like having a rotating filter on a camera lens, amber here, burnt sienna over there. While there were cars on the road, people didn't act panicked, they seem to be as much in awe as he was.

The good news was that he hadn't seen any flames, yet. He drove by Joshua Florini's office in hopes that he might have some insight not available to the public, yet. The parking lot was empty. He drove toward the north end of town on The Ridgway, then cut over to Starke and back down south; past the Albertson's grocery store, the Dollar General, McDonald's, the Safeway and all the way down past Benson Road. The further east he traveled, the darker it got; the smokier it was, but he was glad to not see any flames. He turned around on Easy Street and made his way back north. At the intersection where Starke crossed Benson, he was now seeing a fairly steady stream of vehicles moving west on Benson, away from the fire, as he waited for the light his direction to change green.

It was so hard to know how to react. James considered himself pretty level-headed in times of crisis, of course, having lived through more than his fair share of them probably had something to do with that. Experience, good or bad, was a great teacher. What he really needed was information. He didn't know whether to stay and try to be of help, or just get off the hill and out of the way. With cell towers down, he had no data save the ever-growing, ever-evolving plume of smoke. It had expanded to a point that widthwise (north-south) it was all-encompassing from his vantage point. He could still see the front edge of it as it expanded across the town from east to west, but it stretched as far as he could see in the other three directions.

When the light changed and the cars in front of him began to creep forward, James made the split-second decision to turn into the massive parking lot of Ace Hardware, which was situated on the Southeast corner of that intersection. As he pulled in, he drove to the farthest corner, away from the building and parked near the street. He climbed out and saw that a few of the employees of the hardware store were standing outside watching the smoke and chatting nervously. James also noticed the tiny bit of irony that three of them were smoking cigarettes at the time.

James walked out to the street corner; the westbound light was green so he waited for a few minutes until the light turned red. He noticed the giant American flag hanging from, at least, a forty-foot pole at the Chevron across the street. It wasn't simply flapping in the wind, but was audibly snapping from the tension, as a corner of it would snap against the taut main fabric. Once the line of cars came to a stop, he crossed the crosswalk. The tails of his untucked shirt were snapping now, like the flag. Upon nearly reaching the other sidewalk he turned abruptly and walked between the two lanes of stopped westbound cars.

"You guys okay?" He asked the first couple of cars, hoping to get some to engage. They didn't.

He kept walking, "Are you evacuating?"

A teenager in an older little Chevy S-10 finally replied, "I thought I was going to work, then got pulled into all the traffic. Is the fire big?"

Clearly, he wasn't going to have any answers. James kept walking. There were plenty of cars. Still, most of the drivers seemed calm and stoic.

He came to a minivan and recognized the young lady driving it. He didn't know her, didn't even know for sure where he knew her from, that's kind of how small towns work; you vaguely know most everyone, even if you don't really know them. She looked up and her eyes smiled in recognition. She rolled down the window.

"Hi," she said with a smile.

James guessed she was in her mid to late twenties. He could see the edge of at least one car seat through the tinted back slider. Cute girl, though she never really put much effort into it. But she had a nice smile and had always seemed friendly enough, even to familiar 'strangers'.

"Hi, how are you? Where are you coming from? Just trying to get an idea if the fire has climbed up to the ridge, yet."

"I didn't see any, but when I let the dog out this morning, I saw the smoke. I just decided to pack everyone up and go spend the day at my mom's house."

"Were, you out on the canyon, or where are you coming from?"

"No, I lived down off Edgewood. I think it'll be okay. I just didn't want the baby breathing all this smoke."

"I hear ya," James replied. "Good Luck, good job looking out for those kiddos. Hopefully, they'll get this knocked down and you guys will be back home by dinnertime. Good to see you, Thanks."

The light turned green, she waved as she drove off. James made his way over to the safety of the sidewalk as the rest of the cars followed her lead.

Thursday 7:54 am – NIFC, Boise, ID

Fire Chief Joey Oliver stood near the back of the National Interagency Coordination Center (NICC), looking at a real-time satellite infrared image of the Sawtooth mountains on a computer.

The National Interagency Fire Center is the nation's support center for wild-land firefighting. The center provides a number of services for the men and women tasked with fighting the ever-growing number of wildfires. Funded primarily through the Bureau of Land Management (BLM), they provide a great deal of analytical data and predictive models to aid in prevention. The NIFC also offers extensive programs of training and coaching best practices and safety of those going into harm's way to manage and/or fight wildfires from a national perspective. It also has a role in logistics and support of both men and equipment. This was handled in the NICC.

Joey looked around the table. He was currently the senior man on the premises, and as such, was tasked with finding ways to help those fighting what incident commanders and news anchors alike were calling the BonnFire.

Wildfire naming conventions dictate that an incident is named a distinctive name based on the actual origin of the fire. The fire screaming towards Genna had started in a field off of Bonneville Road. Some jokester had gotten lazy and decided that Bonneville Fire was too much of a mouthful, so they shortened it to BonnFire. Joey just knew that because of that choice, half of the population of the United States would never read beyond the headlines and would forever assume some high school kids had built a big bonfire and it got out of control.

There were seven others in the NICC at the moment trying to figure out how to best help assist the firefighters on the ground, in Genna.

"John, what's the chatter from the helos?"

"There are three choppers in the area, but they have all grounded at what used to be the airport in Rome. The winds are simply too extreme. From the air, because of the way this smoke flume has formed and reacted to the winds, they simply have no visibility. They cannot see the fire itself; they would be blind drops. The pilots all insist that they would fly if they knew they could hit their targets, but the dangerous conditions are too great for release and pray shots."

"Would a fixed-wing supertanker fare any better?"

"Slightly, they would be able to fly above the

wind until they swoop down to make their drops. However, because of their greater speed, they need visual markers even more than the helicopters. At any rate, all of the supertankers are at least three hours out at the moment."

The irony was not lost on Joey, that here they were, incredibly lucky that the NIFC was located right here in Idaho, a mere ninety miles from Genna and yet... there was very little that they could do to help. The weather gods needed to cooperate.

"Get the supertankers in the air and on the way, if we get a break in the wind, I want them to do blind drops, if necessary, right along that ridge, at least we might be able to slow this thing down."

"Hey Chief, you're going to wanna look at this!" cried one of the tech guys. He punched a few buttons and the Infrared satellite image appeared on the large main screen in the front of the room.

"Okay, I am going to roll this back twenty seconds, see if you see what I saw."

The image on the screen, replete with red, blues, green and black showed the front line of the fire stretched nearly ten miles wide about halfway up the slope to Genna. There were also a few small tracks of the rear flanks that had grown some, but they weren't as worrisome as the wind-driven front. Suddenly on the screen, the front fire line flared and pulsed. Instantaneously, atop the ridge, several dozen small spot-fires appeared.

"What the fuck was that?"

Fire Chief Oliver knew exactly what it was. He had only witnessed it once before in his career. Something that you really don't want to happen in a forest fire.

The BonnFire had gone airborne.

"Ok, we may not be able to get help to them in time to save Genna, but scramble every available unit from the western US, Oregon is closest so start there. John, you call the Bear County Fairgrounds in Rome. We're going to take it over... that will be our command center. We need to give them everything we've got, or we're going to lose half the state of Idaho. Let's move."

Chapter Four

Thursday 8:01 am – Genna, ID

Tristan Byrne and two of his crew were working a street where several of the airborne firebombs had landed, on what they hoped was the northern edge of the front. It was a nice upper-middle-class neighborhood, but like most of the areas in Genna, with a canyon view, it was a mixture of contemporary upscale homes and sixty-year-old cottages left over from the days when this was an area to escape to on weekends. Four houses were burning. He had six men and two trucks. He left four to begin fighting the first two burning homes that they came to, while he and the other two began running up the street knocking on doors. There were only a handful of families loading up to leave. Where was everyone else? Had they already fled? Were they out of town? Were they still asleep?

He had a bullhorn, but they'd left the siren on in his truck in the hope it might rouse someone. This, unfortunately, made the bullhorn next to useless. He knocked on the first door, pounding loudly. No response. He pounded a few more times. Then he moved on to the next house. No response. Across the street, his buddy Tim had had more success at his first few houses. Two older couples had been asleep still and woke to a horrific scene. Tim told them to go change clothes, grab any animals and get in their cars. There was no time for anything else. They needed to move.

Tristan pounded on the next door. No response. Could all the people on the canyon side, have been watching the fire's progress and already gotten out? It was feasible. But something felt wrong. He glanced back at the blazing homes and said a silent prayer that they had already been gone too. The first four were fully engulfed now and had spread to two more. His guys on the hoses were fighting a losing battle. He watched as a burning branch from a neighbor's home detached and dropped onto the roof of the first home he had knocked on. The branch slid down the pitch of the roof and came to rest on the corner of a rain gutter. Full of pine needles and leaves the gutter ignited and ran a line of fire all the way across the front of the house. He dropped the bullhorn where he stood and sprinted back down towards that first house, determined not to let it burn. He raced up the driveway and as he hit the first step on the porch, he launched himself into the air and just managed to reach and grab onto the rain gutter with his gloved hands, hanging on like he was finishing a slam dunk in the NBA. Now he was in a quandary, he had expected that his body weight would rip the gutter from the eave that it was attached to. Instead, it held, though the metal where he had gripped it was bending, it left him dangling like last year's Christmas lights. He jerked his body a couple of times hoping the bouncing action might pull it away, but no, the metal near his hand simply bent some more. He shuffled his hands a bit over to the right, to where he had a stiffer edge to grip. Despite the fireproof gloves, he could certainly feel the heat on his fingertips. He swung his feet up and planted his boots on the wall. He took a deep breath, knowing this was a bad idea, then shoved off the wall with all his might, using the strength in his legs to rip the gutter from its mount and sending him flying backwards and dropping him eight feet down, flat on his back. He landed awkwardly half on the sidewalk, half on the grass, the impact expelled all the air from his body and the gutter rained burning debris all over him. Tim's face appeared in his line of blurry vision, and before he knew it, he was on his feet and Tim was brushing hot embers from around his face and neck. As his breath returned to him, Tristan looked across the front of the house; his acrobatic act had worked, all but the last hanger had pulled free.

"Well, that was stupid." He declared flatly to Tim.

"Ya think?"

Tristan wandered over and yanked the last one free, sending the gutter to the ground with a thump and bringing the branch that had started it all down with it.

"Win number one for the good guys."

The two headed back over to the rest of the team to check-in and come up with a plan. When they reached the other guys, they looked utterly defeated: dripping sweat, dragging their feet. Tristan looked around. At least four more spot fires had sprung up along this stretch of road, engulfing another house at the far end of the road. It felt like hell, but Tristan knew this was going to get much worse before it got better. They simply didn't have the manpower or resources they needed. Hell, he would normally have more guys than this fighting a single home fire, and the other teams stretched all along this canyon, he was certain, were just as baffled. And the actual front line of the fire hadn't even arrived yet. They needed to take a different tack. Tristan realized what they needed to do. He gathered the guys around him, like a quarterback in a huddle.

"Chins up guys, this is just a warmup. We were a little slow getting going, but we need to put that behind us." He looked around, to see that he had their attention. "Take a deep breath. Then we switch gears, we will all focus on clearing these houses and getting people evacuated. Let's mask up and go in every structure that we can. Don't bother knocking anymore, take the sledgehammers and get inside. Once we've cleared these, we'll fall back and figure out where Cap wants to draw the line in the sand on this beast. Work together, teams of two. You two and you two will buddy up and work that side of the street." He looked at the next two, "You start here, Tim, you're with me we'll start at the other end of this side. Got it? Let's save these people."

The guys got the lockboxes opened and each grabbed their tool of choice; sledgehammers, Halligan bars, Jake rakes, and Tim's favorite the 'Maximus-Rex'. Loaded up and masked up they picked up the pace to go clear these homes. Tristan noticed a few of the folks that Tim had connected with were making their way to their cars, though one guy was going down the street knocking on neighbors' doors trying to rouse anybody that he could.

Suddenly, the sky around them erupted with what first appeared to be a meteor shower against the deep black sky. Clusters of fiery debris came down in droves, as if a dragon had sneezed and bits of fire scattered everywhere. Numerous trees burst into flames; roofs ignited. The wind roared.

The firefighters all picked up the pace. Tristan ran straight to the civilian that had been knocking on doors. He had taken refuge under the overhang above a neighbor's front porch. Not a bad spot, but then again he couldn't see that the roof above him had started burning. Tristan waved him towards him and when they met, he put an arm around his back and tried to keep his head low to help shield him from the still raining embers.

"You need to go now!" Tristan yelled over the suddenly very noisy scene. "Which one is yours?" The man pointed to his wife running to the car, with her purse hooked onto and elbow and a cat held tightly between her crossed arms. Tristan ran him all the way to the car. "Don't stop, get out of the area! We'll get your neighbors." The man paused to look at his home, likely for the last time. Tristan nudged him back into action and pushed him towards the car.

"Go, go, go, NOW!"

Once the man was in the car, Tristan turned to rejoin Tim who had just reached the second to last house – their starting point, since the house on the end was fully engulfed now. The roof was burning, but Tristan didn't think that the fire had broken through to the attic, yet. Tim was struggling to get the door opened with the Halligan bar alone.

Tristan ran up behind him and yelled, "Watch your hands!" Tim moved his hands just as Tristan came down on the bar with a mighty swing of the sledgehammer. The door hopped on its hinges as the deadbolt ripped out through the inner door frame. Tristan shoved the door open a stream of dark smoke wafted out onto the porch. Apparently, he had been wrong about the roof fire not breaking through. Smoke alarms were shrilling and chirping throughout the house, but he saw no signs of anyone from the entryway. They walked into the well-appointed home with an open floorplan and hardwood flooring throughout. He cleared the living room, while Tim cleared the kitchen. They made their way to the living quarters. The first door was open; it was an empty guest room. Tim opened the next door in the hallway and jumped back; startled by a gray cat that blew past them both and made its escape out the front door, sliding and almost smashing into the front door frame as its claw's traction failed in the final turn on the way outside. In the bathroom were water, food and a litter box. Apparently, the cat couldn't be trusted to roam the house overnight.

Two more doors were left, both closed. Tim took the one on the right, while Tristan took the one at the end. The smoke was getting heavier, they knew they were almost out of time. Tim opened his door first; an office and craft room of some sort. No people.

Tristan opened his and entered the spacious master bedroom. The smoke was heavier here as it had built up behind the closed door. Tristan glanced up at the ceiling, the discoloration was extreme. He was out of time. Still, he made his way carefully to the Queen-sized four-poster bed. The side nearest him was neatly made and undisturbed. But through the smoke, he could see a shape on the far side. Warily he shuffled around to the other side. A frail-looking lady, she looked to be in her late seventies or early eighties, stared back at him with wide-open blue-gray eyes. But he could see instantly the emptiness of those eyes; death had reached her first. Still, Tristan reached out to her to shake her awake. She didn't wake. In fact, she felt rather stiff, as if she had been dead for a while. That didn't make sense.

Before he had a chance to think any deeper about it, the ceiling succumbed to gravity, bringing burning sheetrock and insulation down on top of the bed. The fresh oxygen in the room combined with the fresh fuel of the sheets and comforter caused the room to burst into aggressive flames. Tim was right there to grab Tristan by the back collar of his fire jacket and pull him backward out of the room. Tristan's gaze never left the lady's open eyes until they were back in the hallway. He snapped out of his trance as Tim all but shoved him down the hallway towards the front door.

"We can't help her now; we need to go help the others. Come on."

Thursday 8:06 am – Genna, ID

Hailey got to the end of Breyer and Pulga road

was packed full of cars, all just in the single lane going up towards where it intersects with the upper section of The Ridgway. Clearly, her neighborhood was evacuating, but slowly, very slowly. Hailey sat there trying to relax, but the burst of adrenaline from waking up panicked in the face of a firestorm makes patience a challenge. Hell, on a good day, if there were more than three cars at Dutch Brothers when she went to get her coffee, she lost her patience. But she was definitely in survival mode. The kids are all crying. She can't see Joe's work truck now; she can only assume that he is in that line.

I'm not going to be the first person to drive on the wrong side of the road, but if someone goes first, I'm going and not getting stuck here.

Right then a car flew by, she quickly pulled out to follow. People in other cars are honking at her, flipping her off, calling her a bitch, and worse. But she had two nine-year-olds, a two-year-old and a five-month-old in the van with her. After a half a mile she was forced to turn left onto gate lane, which was empty, thankfully. She sped down that lane and turned left, at the end, onto southbound Starke Road which was also empty at the time. Zero cars were going up or down the hill; which was highly unusual. She reached for her phone to call Joe and find out where he was, but then remembered that it had fallen off her nightstand. She had never even thought to grab it. Shit!

As she approached the next light a few other cars materialize, people were still using the light fairly normally. Waiting for their lights to change. Right before Hailey's turn people start to panic and a surge of cars swarm in from the eastern crossroad. Nearly instantly, everything was gridlocked and no one was moving. She looked to her left and through the darkness and the smoke she saw a solid wall of flames the length of the canyon.

It was here! Still a distance away, but the fire had reached Genna. The BonnFire certainly did not look like a bonfire; but more like a tidal wave created by the combustion fury and evil. Hell had come to Genna, yet, many of her residents were not even aware that their paradisiacal bliss was threatened.

Thursday 8:10 am – Rome, ID

Michael pulled his car into the parking lot of a Starbucks at the base of The Ridgway. He parked at an angle which gave him the best view up the hill, towards home. After being stopped in his attempt to get up Deal Road, he had tried the other two routes into Genna, as well. He racked his brain trying to come up with another solution. Despite his view of the Ridge, which from his vantage point looked more like an active volcano with the large plume of smoke spreading across the entire area now, he still thought that they were in pretty good shape.

They lived in an older two-story, two-bedroom house on the southwest side of Genna. It was a cute little place, two-tone blue-gray walls, and trim, a redwood stained wooden deck serving as the front porch, that also connected to the side door of the detached garage. It was cozy, but it was home. The fire was coming from the east/northeast, they lived in the southwest. He didn't fear for the house, there was no way the fire would burn that far into town. He wasn't even terribly concerned for the pets, except that if the evacuation held, they would miss their dinner tonight and the dogs would probably crap in the house. No, his greatest fear was about to be on the other end of the phone in his hand. He was mostly sitting here and stalling, before letting Christy know that after stopping her from going back up the hill, he had failed to rescue them himself.

He could now see a steady stream of traffic coming off the hill, much heavier than the normal commute into work. State Troopers were at each intersection along this stretch, ostensibly to keep traffic moving, but somehow that wasn't happening. From where he was sitting, Michael was only eleven miles from his house. Unfortunately, with canyons on both sides, there only four roads, or evacuation routes off of the hill: Pulga, Starke, Dean, and The Ridgway. Additionally, The Ridgway was the only route out traveling further uphill and to the north. The trek around to try to get in that way would take him at least three hours. It just didn't seem like a viable option when he was quite sure that they were still going to have that route closed off too. He was going to have to just face the music and pray for a good outcome. He hit the call button on his phone.

"Hi, where are you? Did you connect with your Mom?" He asked as light-heartedly as he could.

"Yeah, we're just filling up with gas at Costco. Lots of people are beginning to congregate here from Paradise. How'd it go with the animals?"

"It didn't." He paused waiting for a reaction, but he got nothing. "I got turned around by checkpoints on every road in... so frustrating. But please, try not to worry. They'll be fine. The fire is on the other side of town. Hopefully, like last time, they'll lift the evacuation orders tomorrow morning and we'll go check on them. Worst-case, we have to clean up some poop on the floor." He was rambling, by now, just talking to keep her from envisioning the real worst-case scenario.

Denial was a very powerful force, especially when you really, really wanted to believe in something, like that what he had just described to her was probably the best-case scenario. Even Michael wasn't ready to contemplate the real worst-case.

But Christy simply replied, "Okay, come find us in the Costco parking lot."

Michael had to admit that that nonchalance was unexpected. And frankly, it scared him.

"Okay, on my way."

Thursday 8:12 am – Genna, ID

Sheriff Ezra Horne had stayed to make sure the hospital evacuation was off to a good start, now he was trying to get across town to Town Hall to get and give a status update with the Town Manager and Mayor, he hoped the GPD chief would be there too. As he turned onto Benson, he realized he had a whole other set of problems.

The fire had crested the ridge just as he was leaving the hospital, but from here it seemed the southern flank had made inroads much faster than the areas that they had initially been most concerned with, it had crossed Pulga and was burning its way up to where he was now, but he and hundreds of people were stuck on this stretch of roadway at a dead stop.

"Why are all these people still here? We need to get everyone off this hill now. Evac everyone now! Who's closest to Benson and Starke? We need to get the westbound lanes open now!" He called over his radio.

"Deputy Harris here Sheriff. I'm on site here now. There's nowhere for them to go. It's jammed up at The Ridgway and we're pushing flow as fast as we can down Starke."

Ezra looked down Edgewood, the only street that he could see down, the far end of the street was fully ablaze casting an orange glow on the homes in front of it. He said a quick prayer.

"Deputy Harris, Listen closely. Stop all other directions of traffic and get Benson moving or we are going to have a catastrophic loss of lives in the next five minutes. Do you understand me?"

As he unkeyed his mic, he decided he had to take charge of this himself. He flicked on his lights and siren and edged his way between the rows of cars, who dutifully cooperated and pulled over as far as they could on a two-lane road with no shoulders. First an inch at a time, then a foot at a time. After a fair distance, he came upon a vehicle, a rather run-down early 80s Chrysler Reliant K car, that was in the middle. It looked like the left lane was clear ahead of him, but the driver appeared wary of driving on the wrong side of the road. Instead, he sat in between, effectively blocking both lanes. After the Sheriff siren and horn failed to move him, the Sheriff got out and jogged up to the driver's window, but the car was empty.

The car behind him yelled out his window, "I think he ran out of gas and decided to walk."

Ezra spun around, "He just left it here? How

long ago?"

"Yeah, like ten minutes ago."

"How long have you been here?"

"In this spot? I got here like a few minutes before that guy left. But it's taken us over thirty minutes to get from Pulga this far."

BOOM! An explosion sounded from behind them, in the direction of the neighborhood down Edgewood, followed moments later by another BOOM! The Sheriff turned, but couldn't see anything. He couldn't even tell if they were electrical transformers blowing or propane gas tanks. Here in the mountains, many people heated their homes with propane gas stored in big tanks on their properties. Though the Sheriff knew that they really didn't change the situation, it was clear that the new noises on top of an already surreal visual situation, with the morning darkness and thick smoke, served to make many of the people jumpier. A number of horns began to blow and several colorful words were screamed from car windows, as the, once patient, evacuees began to lose their cool.

The Sheriff acted quickly, he motioned to the few cars that had him in their line of sight.

"Come give me a hand." He reached into the open window to shift the car into neutral and started trying to turn the steering wheel sharply to the left.

Initially, he thought the steering wheel lock was engaged, but soon realized that without being on, there was simply no power steering. He leaned his right shoulder into the window-frame and began to push. Slowly the wheels began to move and that made turning the steering wheel much easier. A moment later two other guys arrived to put their weight behind the trunk and push. Ezra steered left and as momentum picked up, he steered back right to straighten it out as it went along the edge of a deep drainage ditch. He stopped as the momentum increased even more and fell behind the car with the other two guys and they gave it a final shove dropping it into the ditch, rolled over on its side.

"Thanks, guys." He looked at the large guy with the crew cut and black t-shirt. "Which car is yours?"

"That blue Silverado."

"And you?' He asked the smaller young man with the man bun and purple socks. "This is me right behind where the K car was."

"Okay, When I start down this lane, I want the Silverado to merge into this lane behind me, then you follow me in the Honda, ok?" They both nodded. "I am hoping that the people behind will see you guys merging and do the same."

"Great, stay safe gentlemen." The Sheriff cried as he climbed into his patrol car.

Sheriff Horne moved slowly forward and into the left lane, lights still flashing but the siren was now off. He watched as the Silverado merged into this lane, followed by the Honda and more importantly he saw the two cars behind them do the same thing. It had worked. He had cleared the logjam behind but now had to go figure out how to get these people off this road. He feared that his other title would play an important role here if they didn't get this cleared out. For in Bear County, the Sheriff was also the Coroner.

Thursday 8:15am – Genna, ID

Hailey cried but was trying hard not to let the kids see her fear. The drive down Starke had been slow. They were stopped at a light and had been sitting there for nearly 20 minutes, not moving. But the moment of quiet seemed welcome; the kids had quieted down mostly. The older ones were doing their best to console the little ones. There was no panic now, just an urgent desire to get off this hill. Just as something opened up and they began to inch forward, their situation changed.

Suddenly all of the lights in stores, street lights, and traffic lights all shut off in the same instant. Moments later they started hearing very loud booming noises. That's when she knew it was here. The McDonald's across the street burst into flames, along with the trees surrounding it. The wind whipped seemingly even faster than they had been as the blaze sucked oxygen towards it to help the flames reach unimaginable heights. The fire quickly spread to the next building, a row of small businesses. Despite being only 8:15 on a November morning, the instant rise in temperature caused Hailey to turn the air conditioning on to full blast.

Suddenly, traffic jumped from inch by inch to almost fifteen miles an hour, super slow, but they were grateful to be moving at all. The fire followed them south on Starke. Soon, the encountered a number of fire trucks staged in the northbound lanes. It hadn't occurred to her that she hadn't seen a single fire truck out this morning. It looked like they were going to make their stand here at Starke to try to keep the fire from spreading. As she rolled down the road, they passed the Safeway; its entire shopping center was in flames. Once she almost reached Benson, she could see some guys out in the intersection directing traffic. One she recognized as Sheriff Horne, he had become a larger than life figure in the area since handling a dam collapse scare, last year. She inched a little further and could see that they were letting all the westbound traffic from Benson Road turn to go down Starke while directing all the southbound cars to turn right onto Benson.

At first, she didn't understand, *Wouldn't Starke be faster for all of them?* Then she noticed the condition of the cars from Benson. Many of them had scorch marks along their sides and a few had even had their plastic taillights melt and teardrop down their bumpers. Somehow that made it even more real. These people had almost burnt in their cars. She had had it easy so far, though to her it didn't feel like it.

When she was second in line to turn, she caught a glimpse of the other guy directing traffic... *Is that James? What is he doing out there?*

She watched as another deputy ran up and brought James and the Sheriff face masks, the little white ones with the rubber band strap. She rolled down her window.

"James, James!!" She yelled to get his attention. With the window down, she could really hear the explosions.

"Hi, Hailey are you guys okay? You get everyone out?"

"Yeah, Joe is in his truck but we lost him. What are you doing out here?"

"Whatever I can... It's insane. Be safe. Between you and me, nobody down Benson," he pointed the way she was about to turn, "has seen the flames yet, so they haven't panicked and loaded up the other side. If I was you, I would run up the wrong lane as far as you are able to and get these kids out of here. Good luck, and pray. Pray for all of us."

He stepped back into his position and waved the car in front of her through, then waved her on as well.

Thursday 8:22 am -Genna, ID

Eric pulled into the driveway where his wife and daughter were waiting. The neighbor across the street had come over and told his wife, Stacy, that they were evacuating. Her husband was a law enforcement officer and perhaps had better situational intel. He must have heard it was bad. They and their kids were loaded up and drove off within the next few minutes. Little did Eric know he would never see them again.

He asked his daughter how she got up here because she was supposed to be at work in Rome.

"I heard about the fire and left work and took an Uber up."

"Really? An Uber driver would drive you up the hill into a fire?"

His daughter shrugged at his incredulousness. "I guess so."

The modern world sometimes surprises old people like me.

A couple of neighbors came over to talk. The smoke was getting thicker. They still were getting sunshine, as the sun was low and coming in beneath the smoke. They discussed what was happening.

None of them had any real information. Nobody had received any warnings from the much-touted Code Red automated alert system. Of course, with no power and no cellular coverage, there wasn't much point in sending out text messages, he supposed. There had been evacuations. But, as far as they knew, they were all on the east side of town along the canyon. Clearly, they knew the fire was there, hell, Eric had seen it at the hospital, but that was all the way on the other side of town. Eric told them his theory that they'd have to stop the fire somewhere before it got to them, probably along Starke Road firefighters would make their stand. But they were concerned.

One neighbor hooked up his camper and turned it around to face The Ridgway. Eric, Stacy, and Kersten went into the house to pack. He had been up all night.

"You look tired," Stacy said, "maybe you should lie down and sleep for a couple of hours. If the fire comes it will be a while."

"No, I am too amped. This is crazy. There is no way I could sleep."

Another neighbor pulled up in her car and knocked on the still-open front door.

"Do you guys have any gas? I am almost out."

"Hi Susie, no, I think the only gas I have is for

the lawnmower and it has oil mixed in it. I wouldn't risk putting it in your car. It might stop it."

Stacy chimed in, "Why don't you run up Ridgway to the Chevron, real quick?"

"Thanks anyway, but I already tried that, no traffic is being allowed up Ridgway. It was two lanes going down and two lanes coming up for emergency vehicles only. We have been standing at the end of the street watching the traffic. I saw a bunch of police cars and ambulances. Only a rare fire truck. It's kind of weird."

"I noticed the same thing on the way back from work. Maybe they have them all coming up Pulga since that's the closest to the fire. Either way, you should make a run for it with whatever gas you have, it's mostly downhill from here, Good Luck!" She left; they began loading up the cars.

While in his driveway, some motion caught his eye. The way the sun was dancing on the ever-spreading smoke layer. It was all wrong, but he didn't know why. He walked over towards The Ridgway; they were only three houses down from it. He watched the smoke, trying to identify what was wrong with it. It didn't make any sense to him, but the smoke seemed to be rising out of Salmon River Canyon. There was no fire there. The fire was on the other side of town. How could there be smoke rising up there? He looked to the South, a helicopter carrying water beneath it was flying towards the canyon. It flew to just over the edge, it hovered there for a few moments, then suddenly it veered off and fled without dropping its water. This wasn't good. Firefighting helicopters peering into the canyon and fleeing had to be a bad sign. Had the fire jumped the whole town?

The neighbor with the camper took off. He'd seen enough.

Then all hell broke loose. Explosions sounded off from Salmon River Canyon. One after another. Boom, boom, boom. Hollywood wildfires never had explosions. What in the world was causing all the explosions?

The fire crested the rim of the canyon and suddenly the far side of Ridgway, the west side, was ablaze. This was followed quickly by the near side of Ridgway. Yes, it changed that fast. The fire was moving so quickly that panic seemed logical.

Eric's wife screamed, "We need to go, it's time, we have to run."

There was no more sunshine. It had become night time at eight-thirty a.m. Stacy and Kersten jumped into the newer Subaru. Eric jumped into the older Subaru behind it. Both cars started. Headlights shining through the murk, she drove off into the smoke. Both sides of the road were now on fire. Walls of fire. It was getting warm. Eric followed his wife for about 100 feet to assure her that he was behind her. She disappeared into the smoke. Eric stopped his car, put it into reverse and started backing up.

Thursday 8:33 am – Genna, ID

Hailey turned right onto Benson, with a friendly wave goodbye to James. She immediately followed his advice and got into the other, oncoming, lane since the traffic in the right lane was backed up all the way. She finally took a deep breath and relax a bit. They were moving and she was getting her kids away from the fire. Other cars fell in behind her in the wrong lane. When she was close enough to see the light at Ridgway, a police officer walked out into the street and stopped her. She had no choice. She stopped and rolled down the windows, sensing the tears begin to return. Damnit, she was so close to safety.

"Ma'am, we need to keep this lane clear for emergency vehicles. Get back in line."

"I'm sorry, but my house is gone already, we barely made it this far and I have my babies with me. Please just let me go."

He looked at her. He had tears in his eyes and he backed away from the van and just said, "Go."

She thanked him and left. A minute later she turned left onto The Ridgway, still in the wrong lane, thinking *Omg, we made it; we are safe.* She starts driving down to Rome, with a smile on her face.

Right when she passed the last light and curved around that first little turn... bam! She slammed on her brakes and screeched to a stop behind a snarl of cars and everything she can see was on fire, right up to the edge of the road, even the center median was on fire. Once again, she sat there and no cars were moving. The car in front of her, a black Honda Civic, started to catch fire and still didn't move.

She was watching the majestic dance of flame across the car when an enormous gust of wind shook her van. At the same time, the flame surged with the influx of oxygen from small to huge, much higher than the cars. It was, by any definition, a wall of fire.

All of a sudden, she heard her kids screaming and turned around. Her van was on fire and the kids were trying to get out, saying, "We have to run!"

Instantly, she thought, *I can't run barefoot, with four kids.* "Shit!"

She told them, "Not yet!" and gunned the van to the side of the wrong side of the road. She crushed the gas pedal into the floorboards and drove straight into the wall of fire, and just kept droving through alternating views of pitch black and orange flame. She couldn't see anything, she had no idea what obstacles she might hit, hidden inside the hellish environment. She could see flames coming out the side of the van, just before the side mirrors melted and fell off.

Just drive through it until you can't drive anymore and then run. She cheered herself on.

Finally, she started to see light that wasn't emitted by flame, and soon she could see again. Smoke still surrounded them, but they had made it through. The van was still burning, but she kept her speed up in hopes that it would blow out.

Just then a young boy, about high school age, fell out of the bushes on the median, into the street. He then jumped back up and started running down the shoulder. He looked exhausted and scared. With all her heart, Hailey didn't want to stop. She wanted to keep racing all the way to Rome. To safety. But she couldn't pass him by. She slowed down and stopped next to him.

"Get in," she yelled.

He jumped into the van and they speed off. They both were speechless. In shock, more than likely. She wanted to ask him where he'd come from and what he'd been through, but her brain was still trying to process what they had just done.

A few minutes later, he says, "Pull over, there's my mom," and points to a car parked on the side of the road. Hailey dropped him off, without a word, and drove to Rome.

Thursday 8:45am – Rome, ID

The massive parking lot at Costco was overflowing with cars; many fueling up to be prepared for whatever was next. The tension was palpable. There are indeed times in life when one doesn't know what is going to happen, an anxiety of not knowing what will happen in any given situation in the future. But when people are in shock, as those who had just evacuated were, there is little understanding of what had just happened and even less knowledge about what was happening currently up on the hill.

Despite all that shock, tension and uncertainty, there were a great many hugs spontaneously erupting amongst the survivors, whether they knew each other or not. There were even a few smiles and subdued laughter as people reunited with friends and were forever bonded by the experience that they had just endured.

Michael and Christy were somewhat detached from many of those feelings, as they hadn't had to flee through the flames and run for their lives. But they were very much caught up in wondering, and fearing, what might happen as the day progressed. What the fate of their home, belongings and the fate of their animals were.

"Mike!"

He looked around, trying to see where it came from. Of course, as the second most common name in history, often it wasn't even a call to him, which is part of the reason that he tried to use the full version: Michael. Then he saw Bethany walking between some cars headed their direction. Bethany worked in one of the offices in Josh Florini's office complex. He had gotten to know her a little bit over the years. She approached him and wrapped her arms around him in a great hug.

"Hi, I'm glad to see you. Did you guys all get out safe?" That was a question he would ask hundreds of times in the coming days

Tears began to form in her eyes, "Three of the kids and I are here, and we connected with my mother-in-law, but" her bottom lip trembled just slightly, "I can't find my eight-year-old. He was at school, but they had the road closed and I couldn't get to him to pick him up. Nobody up there is answering the phones."

Wow, she is so much more composed than I would be in that situation. Strong lady.

"I'm sure he'll be okay; I think the evacuation plan had buses going to the schools to get the kids out." He gave her another hug. "I'll reach out to a few people and see if I can find out where they are taking the school kids. Okay?'

"Thank you."

"Did you see Josh this morning, did he get out okay?"

"I don't know, when I passed by, he was out directing traffic on The Ridgway, near the office, at the bottleneck. It was crazy."

"Okay, it was really good to see you. Please, please let me know if you reconnect with your son."

"I will."

"Keep your chin up, it'll all be okay."

Christy and Janet were standing there with a look on their face that said, "what do we do now?" The truth was that Michael had no idea. He was unusually calm and collected given the enormity of the situation. He stared at Bethany walking away and shook his head.

"Thank God, we know where Stuart is and that he is safe. Can you imagine?"

"No," a tear dropped from her right eye and slid down her cheek. "What should we do now?"

"Well, the three of us and Stuart are all safe. There seems to be little use staying here. Why don't you guys go have some breakfast or go hang out at the mall or something? Kill time until we need to pick the boy up. I will work on finding us a hotel for tonight and try to get more information about the status up on the Ridge. I need to do something, but so far my hands are tied because we don't know anything."

Thursday 8:53 am – Genna, ID

Wildfire is a living breathing beast. It breathes oxygen, it consumes fuel and excretes waste. By almost any definition that makes it a living being.

But it is also one of nature's true enigmatic forces. Stunningly beautiful, warming and useful to both man and planet. Learning to harness fire, to tame it, was one of the first giant leaps of mankind. Thinking that it was truly tamed was human arrogance, for it can return to its wild nature at any moment.

Tristan saw the wild nature of this fire up close and watched as the open woodland across the street from him morphed from a dozen or so individual tree crown fires into something different. Something monstrous.

As the disparate fires melded together, in the center of this preserved area of woods, near the center of town, the surrounding fires burned the oxygen that fed the core, bringing the formation nearly to starvation. But wild beasts rarely die without a fight. The central bloom began to draw air in, not from around the flames but drawing oxygen up from its base. Like a tree pulling water from its roots, the plume sucked its vital oxygen up and into the plume, causing a chimney effect. It quickly grew three or four times taller than any blaze around it. As it gained critical mass and created its own wind to feed its new addiction, a wobble occurred. Now generating wind speeds of upwards of one hundred thirty miles per hour, that wobble started to cause the entire structure to rotate. Slowly at first, then faster and faster, growing wider and taller with each breath.

Tristan has seen firenadoes in training and created in a lab. Very few firefighters had ever seen a firenado, simply because of how bad conditions have to be to enable their formation. Usually, the crews got pulled out of a section of wildfire before things got that bad and unstable. They simply had never occurred in a town, yet...

Tristan stared at the horrifying, yet fascinating, development of the whirl. He and his crew were posted right in the middle of Starke Road with the rest of the other eighteen crews that had arrived on-scene so far. Most were fighting the fire on the opposite side of the street trying to keep the fire at bay and hold their line. He and his team had turned to the other side once a few airborne blazes had jumped them. They tried to douse the flames immediately, but they were too hot and too fast. Now, he looked at the twirling beast as it sped up even more. The massive amounts of air that its vacuum effect caused to move toward it literally vaporized the water from the hoses before it could get near the ignition points. It twirled quickly but was still traveling slowly. It edged across the park and alongside the Rite Aid drug store's back wall as it spun and picked up debris which swirled around it like orbiting meteors.

As the beast reached the corner of the store, which had worked to block the wind and slightly caused the firenado to shrink, the near gale force winds reactivated the beast. It grew larger; it sped up. And it began to change direction.

Tristan scrambled his crew, and had them load up the trucks to move, while Tristan sprinted to warn the other crews, "Fall Back, fall back!!" He screamed. But the noise overwhelmed his voice. He kept running trying to get their attention.

Suddenly, he was thrown to the ground as a Chevy Suburban, parked in the Rite Aid parking lot, exploded as its fuel tank submitted to the power of the firenado. Chunks of steel and glass launched in an arc around the vehicle, like shrapnel from a grenade. The firenado absorbed the heat energy from the blast and some of the bits and pieces of shrapnel into the cyclonic structure, making it even more lethal if that was possible.

The sound of the explosion, right behind them, got their attention much more efficiently than Tristan ever could have. Fire crews burst into action, as some started to load up, while crews further down the line turned their hoses on the fire whirl to give their comrades cover.

Thursday 9:02am - Genna-ID

James, still directing traffic on Starke Road and Benson, watched in horror as the firenado formed and took out several cars in the parking lot just a few blocks up the road. Though it was a quarter-mile from this intersection, watching the firefighters scramble was the first time all day that he had felt fear. Sure, he had been fearful for other people trapped in cars and traffic while flames licked the sides of their cars, but he hadn't yet been afraid for himself. Some drivers had commented on how brave James was for staying to direct traffic, but truth be known, he felt totally safe out there in the middle of an asphalt cross, noting around him to burn. In his mind, he was totally safe where he was; until he saw the firenado. That sent a chill down his spine.

Traffic had slowed to a trickle there at 'his'

intersection, though he was certain that other routes were still jammed. He watched the fire crews scramble out of harm's way; he could see the uncertainty on their faces as they struggled to find a good spot to make a final stand. Half the town was burning at this point and stopping it was looking to be unlikely.

A few moments later, a gray SUV came out of the smoke on Benson and stopped in the middle of the intersection and waved James over. "Which way is the fastest way to get off the hill?"

"Well, nobody has gone that way in a bit," James pointed down Starke, "the fire was burning below, but it may have crossed over by now, so, maybe you can get through. Or keep going straight down Benson to The Ridgway and turn downhill from there."

As James turned to point down Benson toward Ridgway, he saw a new plume of smoke coming from the other end. He searched his mind to try to make sense of what he was seeing. There shouldn't be rising smoke down there, the fire was over here. The crystallized when it occurred to him that the other canyon must be on fire now.

Shit! He thought to himself. *That's where my house is.*

He turned back to the driver, "If I was you, I would try to go down the hill here. It looks like things are burning this way now. Good luck."

"I'll give it a shot, thanks."

As the man drove off, James noticed another man, laying in the back seat. *Hmmm, that's odd. Too much smoke, perhaps?*

He shook it off. James needed to figure out what to do. He was of no help here, now that traffic had died. There were massive fires to the east of him, a firenado north of him there had been fire to the south, and now he could see smoke coming from the direction of his neighborhood, west. Should he bail and follow that last guy and just get off this godforsaken hill? Should he try to get over to his neighborhood and make sure his neighbors got out? For a guy that was used to being in control, he had no idea where he was needed or what the right move would be. He had no idea what his next move should be.

James was still calm and business-like, but he simply needed guidance on what to do next. Ultimately, he decided to go get his car from the Ace Hardware parking lot where it still sat. He knew should just get to safety if he didn't have a purpose here. And there was nobody else near this area at all. As he walked back to his car, he said a little prayer that he'd learned at A.A.

"God, grant me the serenity to accept the things that I cannot change. The courage to change the things that I can, and the wisdom to know the difference."

That simple prayer always centered him. It quieted his mind. Allowed him to hear guidance. He started the car and saw the time; it had only been an hour and a half since he was at home, like any other day, and found out about the fire. It felt as if he had been out here all day. He looked up Starke Road from where he was parked and saw only devastation. A tunnel of flame and smoke; a gateway to hell. It was horrifying and fascinating... and moving.

James snapped out of his distracted bewilderment and thought his eyes were playing tricks on him; at the far end of his line of sight, he saw a woman stumble, then catch herself, stand back up and continue to run towards him, down the center of the street, as if attempting to escape the maw of a gargantuan dragon.

He shifted into gear and didn't bother backing out, he drove straight off the curb flooring the accelerator as he plunged into the tunnel of doom. The firenado, thankfully, was moving away; but the girl was dodging flames from both sides. He could see now that she was young, in her teens. Electrical transformers exploded above her raining sparks down on her as she tried to cover her head. He sped faster and then turned left as he skidded to a stop ten yards from her, then reached across and pulled the door handle to push the front passenger door open, just as she reached it. She dove into the car pulling the door closed behind her.

"Ohmygod, ohmygod, ohmygod," she kept repeating as if it was a single word, while she aggressively ran her fingers through her hair, and shook her head trying to make sure it wasn't burning.

"You're okay. Not even smoking," he tried to say with humor, "much."

She stopped and looked at him, for the first time. "Thank you, so much. We have to go."

"I am glad that I saw you, I was just about to leave. You picked a rough neighborhood to take a walk in this morning." He laughed and started to drive away. "I'm James by the way."

"Kylie." She replied, then noticed the direction he was going. "Wait, Stop!"

He hit the brakes as two more transformers blew, showering his car with sparkler-like embers.

"We need to go, now."

"Yes, we do. But that way." She pointed back into the dragon's maw. "I ran to get help, there are five more of us. We were in study hall, working on a class project. Apparently, they forgot about us when they evacuated. We came out and found ourselves locked in the school. We had to break a window to get out. We have to go get them."

"We can't drive through that. There's no way."

"I just ran through it; you just need to drive."

James thought back to his prayer, asking for guidance whether he was needed. God had answered him with a seventeen-year-old girl. A damned, brave seventeen-year-old girl.

"Hmmm, be careful what you ask for." He mumbled under his breath.

"What?"

"Nothing. Buckle up. This could get hairy." He glanced over at her dirty blond hair still smoking, despite his earlier denial. "Sorry, poor choice of words. Hold on!"

He turned around and was just about to punch the gas when the power pole behind him cracked and collapsed. He floored it as he saw the tension on the power lines go taut holding the broken one off the ground. The car lurched forward as a second pole succumbed to a bad combination of fire, tension, and gravity, thus putting an even greater tension on the cables connected to the next.

James focused on the charcoal-colored center of the smoke-filled fire tunnel. The heat had increased rapidly inside the car. The poles behind began to snap in series, one after the other, as if chasing them up the block. The fire tunnel continued to constrict and get tighter and tighter, hotter and hotter until all went dark as they reached the smoky center at the end. James subconsciously held his breath, as he had no idea what obstacles lie hidden amidst the smoke. Kylie buried her face in her hands during the plunge.

Suddenly, they broke through the other side. While still dark as night, the smoke hadn't yet settled to ground level. James kept his speed up for two more blocks before he screeched into the high school's parking lot. He immediately saw the other five kids, sitting in the dead center of the parking lot, well away from anything that was actively burning or might burn.

He pulled up. Kylie jumped out before he even came to a complete stop. One of the girls screamed when she saw Kylie and jumped up to give her a hug.

"Ohmygod, you made it."

James was stuck contemplating this new word that seemed to have emerged amongst teens, but he supposed that if they were mentioning God at all, in this day and age, that was probably a good thing. James stood beside the car watching the group interact; four girls and two guys, including Kylie. For a moment, he considered chastising the guys for letting Kylie take that insane run down the street to find help for them. He would have never done such a thing. But as he watched her interact with them, he could see her strength and composure. She was a natural leader, whether she had identified that in herself yet or not. He decided to cut them some slack; why couldn't she be the hero?

So, he moved on to the next problem to overcome. He looked at his little blue Chevy Cruze. It was going to be a tight squeeze to get them all in. Of course, when the alternative is being burned alive in a fire, he was confident they would figure out a way to make it work.

Thursday *9:07 am - Genna, ID*

Eric and his wife had been married for nearly twenty years. In those twenty years, they had never really had a fight or an argument except during the first month they dated. Part of that is because they are very compatible. The other part is that Eric went out of his way to avoid arguing with her.

He knew that he was going to stay and fight the fire. He had been telling his wife for the, almost, eighteen years that they had lived there that he was going to stay and fight for their home if it ever came down to that. His always wife told him she wouldn't let him stay, that she couldn't let him die. That she would make him go.

In 2008, with the Sawtooth fire, he did end up evacuating and giving in to his wife's pleas... and a direct order from a fireman who told them all to go. Afterward, he felt bad, like a blowhard unmasked, because, after all of those years of saying he'd stay, Eric had left. That wasn't going to happen again. This time there was no wife pleading with him. There was no fireman telling him that he must leave. Also, this time there was an actual fire that he could see, and feel... and hear. The Sawtooth fire got close but, he had never really thought that his home truly at risk. This was different. This was why he had let his wife believe that he was leaving, before backing away through the smoke.

It was black as the night. The street was lit up by flames, by burning trees, by burning bushes, by burning wood chips in front yards. Eric lived three houses down from Ridgway. The house at the corner of his street and Ridgway was burning. Across the street from that corner house; the front yard of that home was burning. He couldn't see Ridgway from where he was standing in the yard. Too much smoke. Too much darkness. He wasn't even aware of the snarled mess of traffic that it had become. Every few minutes he'd hear a siren go up Ridgway. Otherwise, explosions and the snapping of flames in trees and brush were the only sounds.

Eric took stock of the situation. None of the

immediate neighbors' homes were burning yet. Across the street, the homes hadn't burned, but the homes and trees behind those were burning vigorously. The tall pines trees were entirely engulfed; flames spreading skyward into the smoke. The neighbor across the street had no trees in his front yard. Just a car and a PVC picket fence. Eric had only small trees and bushes in his front yard. He thought that if he were to be trapped, he could go out to the middle of the street and lie down and be safe. Kind of an open space between the homes.

He got a flashlight from the car and then debated. Leave the car running or shut it off? If he left it running it could get stolen, or it could ingest so much smoke and ash that it might stop. If he shut it off, what if it doesn't start? Realistically, car theft seemed unlikely. He was alone on his street; the neighbors had all left. The neighborhood had no outlet, just the one street in and out. No one would be coming down this street with the idea that they'd escape. It was a deathtrap. And the only way in, or out for that matter, was already fully ablaze. But he grew up in the city, you simply don't leave your car running there, and expect it to stay where you left it. Old instincts tend to haunt you.

So eventually, he decided to leave the car running. On the street. Away from bushes. He walked around the house in search of garden hoses. He found one in the front, two in the back. But only fifty feet long. A definite disadvantage. He turned all three on.

He went inside the house, where they had a small gun safe. Loaded up it weighed maybe a hundred and fifty pounds. He dragged it out of the closet and out the front door. He then walked over to the car and backed it right up to the front porch. He struggled but got the safe loaded into the hatchback. Then he drove the car back out to the street. Away from the house. Away from the bushes. And let it run.

He pondered getting on the roof. He did have an eight-foot ladder and a twelve-foot roof. Normally, he'd get on the roof using the ladder to sweep pine needles and leaves off the roof. Then he'd gingerly climb down blindly and backward hoping to not fall. He decided under the circumstances that was too risky. If he knocked the ladder over or somehow it fell over, he'd be trapped on the roof. It had happened before. This time there was no wife around to pick the ladder up. He'd be trapped. So, no... no getting on the roof.

More reconnaissance to be done. The left side of the house had a space about six feet wide between the house and a wooden fence. If the house or the fence were on fire, he'd have to make a run through a tunnel of fire to get out. On the right side of the house, there was about a twenty-foot gap between the house and the fence. But at the fence was a huge redwood, a large pine, and a whole bunch of bamboo. If that caught on fire that twenty-foot stretch would be intensely hot. He would have to keep an eye on those escape routes and not get himself stuck in the backyard.

The backyard had two huge pines in the middle, a large shop at the right rear and numerous smaller trees. The fifty-foot garden hose could not make it to the back of the shop. Bad news. The ground was covered in Vinca, an evergreen perennial. *That couldn't burn, could it?* Between the Vinca and the house was about ten feet of cement. On the right side, it was nearly all dirt because they had just had the new septic tank put in. On the left a cement walkway and dirt. Maybe he would have a chance here if it came to that.

He went back out to the front, to his car and stood in the street. The car hadn't been stolen. He was still the only one around. The neighbor's house, diagonally across the street and to the right, was now burning. That it was burning wasn't unexpected, but it was deflating to see nonetheless. Perhaps he had thought that the fire would, magically, pass over that small group of homes; and if he could just be there to put out spot-fires, his home might be saved.

It became apparent that wildfires are more aggressive than simply spot-fires spreading. This fire was systematic. It had come up from the canyon, it had burned across Ridgway, it had burned the houses along Ridgway, it had burned the homes behind Eric's neighbor's house and now it was here. Just across the street.

Suddenly, for the first time today, he had trouble breathing. Up to this point, the smoke had seemed familiar; it smelled of burned leaves, burning wood, and pine trees. He hated to minimize it, but it smelled like a campfire. It had been of no concern other than blotting out the sun and causing his throat to dry out. But the smoke from the neighbor's home was pernicious. Black and inky, it rolled across the street and over him. It smelled of chemicals, of plastics, of unnatural things. It was acrid. It stung his eyes; it burned his throat. It gripped his chest.

Eric gagged and, for the first time, started coughing. All of a sudden, the plan to lay down in the middle of the street and let the fire pass if he couldn't escape seemed fallible. He hadn't considered how toxic the fumes might be. Fortunately, the strong winds continued to blow, and shortly the thick black billows were heading in another direction. The pattern would repeat. Good smoke, bad smoke.

Who would think that you'd get to the point of thinking that burning trees and brush would be good smoke? At least survivable. It would be hard to survive the black smoke for long.

He went and shut the car off. He wasn't sure how

the air filter and the engine would deal with the smoke. Eric also began to realize that maybe he couldn't just wait out the fire. Not if toxic fumes were going to kill him. The car might be the thing that would save his life. Shutting off the car did introduce some other concerns.

First of all, would it start again? It's an old Subaru. Who knows? Second of all what if I dropped the keys? It was dark and the fire and smoke weren't going to make looking for keys any easier.

Plus, with the car off the headlights were off. *With the headlights on any rescue teams coming down the street would know someone was in the area and perhaps stop to help. With the car shut off, it was just another abandoned car in the road.*

So began a structured pattern. He'd go to the car every once in a while, and start it; to reassure himself that it would start and to reassure himself that he still had the keys. He'd let it run to keep the battery charged, then get concerned that the black smoke would choke it out, and shut it off again. For the next few hours, he repeated that ritual over and over. A small sense of orderly conduct in an otherwise chaotic situation.

And what of the rescue teams? He kept hearing sirens going up The Ridgway every few minutes, heading somewhere. But not his street. *Wasn't anyone concerned that someone might be stuck in my neighborhood?*

Over the next few hours, every siren brought him hope and then disappointment. *If a fire truck came down my street, they'd see me and help me save my home. They'd see how much it meant to me.*

It did mean a lot, enough for him to be here, in the smoke, all alone. Fighting what would soon be known as Idaho's deadliest wildfire, in history.

Armed with three garden hoses. And a flashlight.

Chapter Five

9:14am - Genna, ID

James was momentarily struck with uncertainty. The fire surrounded them and he was aware that at least two of the four evacuation routes out of town were now inaccessible... at least from here at the school. Pulga Road was all but gone; clearly, with all the electrical poles down, he couldn't try to make his way back down Starke. He wondered if it might be better for them all to stay where they were, but the smoke was so thick that he knew that if the fire didn't get them, the smoke would.

"Let's get loaded up and find a way out of here."

The teenagers crammed themselves into the Cruze. Luckily, though one of the guys was a bit portly, most of them were quite slim. They wedged themselves three-across with two more on laps in the backseat, while Kylie retook her place in the front.

"Look," James said, looking back at the kids via the rear-view mirror, "I'm not going to lie, this is likely to be somewhat terrifying. Know that I will do everything in my power to get you safely off this hill.

But, in order to do that, I need to be able to concentrate and focus. Screaming hysterically will not be helpful in any way. You guys have handled things pretty well so far, but I need you to be brave for just a little bit longer. Can you do that, please?"

Kylie looked back at them, "We can do this, okay guys? What James and I just went through was insane, to get back here. I cannot imagine it getting worse than that."

James cringed at that last line, for he suspected that they were about to face their fears and test their limits. Clearly, this was where he was meant to be.

He pulled out and turned left to run north and cut across to The Ridgway. He knew they couldn't run back the way he and Kylie had just come. Though the areas all around were burning, the flames hadn't encroached the street nearly as much as it had below them.

They made it the short distance to the cross street without incident before turning left. About a quarter-mile down is where things changed; and not for the better. It was a narrow two-lane road and soon the burning structures on either side began to close the gap.

James had a quick bout of deja vu, just as they passed a large Ponderosa Pine, it collapsed, dumping its flaming top half across the road behind them. James knew he had screwed up, he had been paying attention to the structures; people's homes which was horrifying and heartbreaking, but not necessarily dangerous to them. Luckily the tree that had grabbed his attention was behind him. He could see his knuckles turning slightly white as he gripped his steering wheel just a bit tighter than he normally would. He had responsibility for these kids' lives now. Stress was growing within his normally calm mind, anxiety... hell, even a dose of fear if he was honest with himself. With eyes glued to the trees ahead, he carried on. The sound of six kids breathing heavily mingled with the blower fan of the car's air conditioning to create a surreal 'white-noise' backdrop with which his eyes took in the destructive artistry that was on display.

Ahead on the right, he saw another tree begin to topple. He stopped with more than enough room, but now he needed to make some tough decisions. They were hemmed in front and rear by downed trees with only a few hundred yards in between. James had seen a side street on his right, but he thought that was one of the cul-de-sacs that pepper this area, but he couldn't be sure because all the landmarks that would tell him exactly where he was were aflame. He simply couldn't risk driving into the face of the fire and getting stuck, if he had to turn around. He really only had one choice. He said a little silent prayer.

"Okay, you guys underneath, get your seat-belts

on. Then you need to wrap your arms around the others and become their seat-belts. We're going off-road for a bit."

He heard some groaning as they maneuvered to buckle up and get situated and was rewarded by three clicks from the back seat.

"Are you ready?"

More shuffling sounds, then, "Ready!" several of them answered in unison.

James cranked the wheel ninety degrees to the left, to the south. Dropped his smoking little Cruze into first and eased up over the curb. The wooden fence between the properties was already mostly burned, so he planned to just drive through the yards, and hopefully the yards across the next street. He knew if he got past there, he would reach the cemetery. He hoped that the cemetery's open landscape of manicured grass and few trees would be a sanctuary of safety amidst this firestorm. What he wasn't certain of was what the fences or walls around the sides of the properties. He knew that the front was brick and wrought iron, he sincerely hoped that they had skimped on costs, and the back and sides were less robust.

They bumped and thumped between the first set of houses with comparatively little incident. The not-quite completely burnt four-by-four fence posts caused a hell of a racket on the underside of the car, but no noticeable damage. They ejected through the front yard with a big drop off of the raised gravel landscape into the street below, where James came to a stop.

The houses on this street were burning profusely in varied shades of orange, yellow, red, blue and green. The gap between the two infernos in front of them looked similar to the path they had just been on, but with significantly more flames... and a chain-link fence.

"Crap." He turned right to drive past the next house, knowing that every second they wasted put them in more mortal danger. The next house had chain-link too. Those steel posts don't burn. Then he realized that many today are aluminum, not steel, and should collapse when he hit them. So, not ideal, but possible. He drove to the next house, where he saw two fences: one wooden and one chain link, splitting the gap between the houses. The wood side looked to be slightly too narrow for his car, making it likely that he would clip some poles with his front right bumper. But he was out of time. If they were going to stand a chance of surviving the day they needed to get to the relative safety of the cemetery. He would worry about the next move once he got there.

"Kylie, I want you to duck down low into your seat and bring your knees up to your chest. I want you protected in case anything comes through the windshield. But keep your feet off the dashboard, the impact may set off the airbags. Got it. Hold on, guys. Here we go!"

Because of the deep drainage ditch along the front of the property, James entered the driveway on a diagonal to cut across the front yard and turn up along the side of the house and make a run at the wooden fence. As soon as he rounded the corner, he floored the accelerator and aimed at the wooden fence which was mostly on fire.

The impact was violent and noisy. Flaming wooden shrapnel exploded over the car, but the loudest sound came from the collision of the right front bumper with what must have been a steel fence post, not an aluminum one. The right front of the car went airborne a few inches as it rode up onto the post before the post gave out and folded over, but not without ripping the plastic, burning, front bumper cover off and letting the tire grab it and pull it under the car where it scraped and bumped until ejecting from the rear. The second pole triggered the airbags, and though James had kind of expected that to happen, you can never really prepare yourself for that kind of explosion. Dazed and with his view blocked completely, James somehow kept his foot on the gas pedal and plowed through the remaining barriers into a clearing, for a moment of relative silence. BOOM! Still blinded by the airbag, they rammed through the wrought iron fence of the cemetery. He eased to a stop.

He didn't know whether to cheer out loud that they had survived or to curl up in the fetal position and cry. He didn't know if he was clinically 'in shock', but the last hour had been a hell of a roller coaster ride. It wasn't over either, but he had a momentary reprieve. He shoved the deflated airbag out of his face and looked around. Kylie was digging out from under her own airbag. The kids in the back were sobbing quietly.

"Is everyone okay?"

The kids all nodded, all completely at a loss for words. James knew this was tough on them, but they were close to some semblance of safety... he thought. The truth was, he had no idea if it was any better, or any more safe, anywhere on this God-forsaken hill. No, he corrected himself, definitely not God-forsaken, for they were still alive. God must be looking out for them because hell nearly had them in its grasp.

He climbed out to the car to assess the situation. The black smoke was thick and heavy, but he didn't see any active flames for at least a hundred yards. That was the largest safe zone he'd seen in what felt like ages. He walked around to the front of the car to see the damage. He wished he hadn't; he'd felt more confident in their survival and escape when he was staring over the hood from the driver's seat. The front bumper was gone, the chromed plastic grill was melted and drooping, the paint on the front half of the car was bubbled and blackened. The radiator was steaming and leaking from both hoses and one spot in the center of the coils. Both headlights were cracked and one was hanging from its wiring harness. The engine was also making a knocking sound that he hadn't heard before. He sighed. They needed to get the hell off this hill, and soon.

He checked the landscape; he could see the American flag still flying inside the gates to the east of him. Somehow even with all the smoke and wreckage that gave him hope. It also let him know that if he could get to the fence a few hundred yards to his right, west, he would be able to break through to Ridgway and hopefully find some help and safety.

Thursday 9:27 am – Bear County, ID

Graham had been watching the development of the fire on Facebook. They didn't have cell service but his internet was still on at the house. They lived on half an acre just outside the northern town limits of Genna. Once he saw it breach into Genna, he and mobilized into action. They had a game plan and were well organized. Frankly, their evacuation would have been simple, comparatively, if they didn't have the horses. They owned three of them, they were stabled on a property in Southeastern

Genna by the airport. Otherwise, from their location, the easiest evacuation route was just to take The Ridgway north and continue uphill and around to the other side of the Salmon River valley before turning back south and going back down towards Rome. His wife, Holly, was an animal lover. They had accumulated nine cats at the house, some of them feral, in addition to the horses down the hill.

They quickly loaded Holly's car, a green Toyota Rav4, with all the valuables: electronics, guns, jewelry, a metal file box with documents, passports, pink slips, and other important paperwork. They also packed enough clothes for them for a few days.

The plan was for Holly to take this car through Genna, down to let the horses out of their stables. Meanwhile, Graham and their 14-year-old daughter would round up all the cats, get them crated and load them into the SUV. They would then evacuate out the northern route and meet in Rome in a few hours.

They all hugged and Holly took off for the stables. Less than two miles, down The Ridgway, the plan began to fall apart. With the vast majority of people trying to go down the hill, and The Ridgway being both the most direct and the furthest away from the fire, it had become a parking lot. Fed from dozens of side streets, there was simply no way to move this many people down the hill. To make matters worse, about three years ago the current

Mayor, Joanna Moody, had been in her first term on the Town Council when they had decided to narrow The Ridgway to one lane each way as it passed through the downtown district to allow for more storefront parking along that stretch. This created a bottleneck during busy times on the best of days, Holly couldn't imagine the impact that bottleneck would have on a day like today. Still, if she could just crawl down a few more blocks she might be able to cut across to Starke Road and go down that way.

Holly briefly considered just turning around and joining her husband and daughter on the longer, but easier evacuation route, but she simply couldn't abandon the horses. She may not be able to tow them anywhere, but she knew that if she let them out of the stables, they would find a way to survive. They would round them up again over the next few days.

But first, she had to get there.

She crept forward, inch by inch. When she rounded the next curve, the scene defied words. Flames were licking cars from both sides as the whole route seemed to be afire. She could see one fire engine with hoses alternating between spraying the roadside fires, then swinging back to hose down cars trying to escape at far too slow of pace to be successful. One car was a burnt-out hull, several more had people running from them, leaving their cars in the middle of the road.

A loud knock on her window snapped her out of her detached viewing mindset and she nearly jumped through the roof. It was a Sheriff's deputy.

"Ma'am, are you physically able to walk?"

"Yes, but it's a long way."

"Ma'am, I am going to ask you to pull over as far as you can and walk down the very center of the street as rapidly as possible. About a half a mile down, there is a Walgreens that is so far untouched, please join the others in the parking lot and we'll find a way to get you down the hill."

"But I have to get to our horses..."

"Ma'am, you need to get out and start walking right now."

As if on cue, the trees to her right burst into flames, while she was looking the other way at the deputy. She gathered her personal strength, grabbed the metal box with important papers and passports before she got out of the car and headed down the hill. Others joined her at the center of the road, as the deputies continued urging people to walk. The heat and smoke were oppressive. But she could see now, that if she didn't look out for herself first, she would never reach the horses.

A short way down, one of the firefighters sprayed a hose over her as he targeted flames on the other side of the road. The heavy mist that settled over her felt good, really good as it cooled the air. *Keep walking*, she told herself, *Walgreens isn't that far.*

She glanced back before rounding the next bend and saw that her car was now in flames. Shortly, she passed an older lady sitting on a rock, next to a burnt-out pickup truck. Her arms held her knees to her chest as she just rocked back and forth as her mind tried to escape the horror. She wasn't crying but was clearly incoherent or in shock. Holly slowly veered over to talk to her.

"Are you okay, hun?"

No Response.

In the gentlest tone she could muster, Holly asked, "Can you walk? Why don't we walk together? They are sending a bus for us soon, we just need to make it a little further, down to Walgreens." She reached out her hand. Finally, the lady's eyes shifted and made eye contact.

"I was on my way down to the store; I didn't know there was a fire. Now Stanley is dead. Why didn't they notify us? Why didn't we know? Why Stanley? What am I supposed to do now?"

"Oh sweetie, come with me. I'm so sorry about Stanley, but we need to keep moving. He would want you to live." She grabbed the stranger's hand and helped her up, put an arm around her and began subtly guiding her into motion.

"How long were you married?"

"Which time?"

"To Stanley?"

Finally, something resembling a laugh occurred. "Nah, buried my last one in 2004. Stanley ain't my husband, he's my truck. Stanley and I have had each other since he was new in 1983. He was the only damn man I ever needed, too."

"Well, okay. Let's get out of here, okay? I am Holly, by the way."

"Phyllis."

"Ok, Phyllis, stick with me. We're going to be just fine."

Thursday 9:32am - Genna, ID

Tristan and his crew were doing their best to protect the evacuation route down Ridgway, but even that seemed a losing battle. He'd fought fires much of his adult life but still couldn't come to terms with the magnitude of what was going on here. Fire ringed them, most of the homes he had seen were gone. The department had abandoned the idea of protecting homes and retreated to protect the five-mile stretch of Ridgway through town, but the traffic simply wasn't moving fast enough. The Ridley

Market shopping center was still standing, they had parked at the edge of the parking lot and were spraying down the areas across the street. The water pressure in this area had dropped significantly, forcing them to utilize the single tanker truck that they had which was still full. Therefore, to protect evacuees, they fired short bursts of water onto the trees across the way and then the cars occasionally to slow things down. This was akin to a soldier that was trapped at the front lines but was down to his last magazine of ammunition.

Suddenly, about twenty-five yards to the north of him, an explosion sent brick and wrought iron flying, as a flaming car crashed through the wall above and screamed down a short hill before leaving the ground momentarily, as it launched into the air before slamming to the pavement and skidding to a stop, narrowly missing a couple of pedestrians.

Tristan and one of his guys both rotated their hoses to spray the sedan down, giving it more than a burst in an attempt to see if anyone was even in it. The second the water was shut off, all four doors opened and Tristan counted as four, five, six, seven people clamored out of the car. The five in the back ran straight over to Tristan's fire truck. The driver and front passenger both stood next to the car and watched, for a moment. The driver was dripping wet, as his window must have blown out at some point, the hoses drenched him as they put out the flames on the car. The driver turned to look at the young girl standing beside him, then they simply laughed out loud, before they turned and walked toward the others by the truck. Tristan could read the man's lips... "I can't believe we survived, haha, ha, ha."

Tristan wanted to cheer the good fortune that these people were okay, but reality held him back... it wasn't over yet. Still, they obviously had a fabulous story to tell.

Thursday 9:42am - Genna, ID

With his neighbor's house across the street and to the right burning, Eric knew he was in for a battle. He had established a pattern. He had opened up the gates on both sides of the house and continually walked around the house; around the back, up the side, across the front, and back into the back. By now there were enough falling burning embers that he had small fires to put out. No big deal. The three garden hoses and he would get around the house about every two minutes and that let him catch the spot fires while they were still small. The three garden hoses covered the area around the house well but did not stretch much further. Occasionally he'd climb the stepladder at the back of the house and peek up on the roof to see that no fires were starting there. So far so good.

On one of his loops, Eric came out to the front and noticed that right across the street that the neighbor's stand-alone basketball hoop in front of his garage was now on fire. He thought it odd that his basketball ball hoop would be burning but not his house. A few minutes later his house was on fire too. It had spread from the other neighbor's house. Now looking across the street it was a wall of fire. The neighbor's house across the street and to the left still wasn't burning but the trees in his front yard had started. Eric tried to stretch the garden hose across the street and put the trees out. The hose only reached about three-quarters of the way across the street. He could get some spray on his trees but not much. Eric felt bad for him. He had moved in only a few months before. Eric had finally met him about four weeks ago when he came over as Eric worked on a project in his front yard. He had moved up here after having his home burn down in the Santa Rosa, California fire in 2017. His aunt had bought the home recently but hadn't moved in, so she let him live there since he was homeless. Eric did offer the requisite joke that all of us were safe now because what are the odds that he'd be burned out twice? He really wished that he had a longer garden hose. He really wanted to try and save his new friend's home. Two times losing everything in a fire seemed to be two times too many.

The smoke was thick, occasionally rancid with chemicals and it was very warm. Eric's throat was dry and he was incredibly thirsty. He had been very active in the heat and had had nothing to drink since leaving work in the morning. But Eric wasn't going back into the house for a drink. Not with the houses across the street on fire. He figured the way people die in fires is to get trapped. He wasn't going to risk going into his house, only to discover that his way out had disappeared. This fire had moved amazingly fast. It could not be trusted. He looked at the garden hose. Eric hadn't taken a drink out of a garden hose since he was a kid. But it was his only viable choice. He took a drink. Forty-five years of garden hose technology and the water still tasted just as plastic and chemically as he remembered from his childhood. You would expect that, in almost fifty years, they would have fixed that. But he drank until he was full. As he gulped away, he thought to himself, it would be ironic to survive this fire but to die of cancer I'd gotten from the garden hose chemicals. One thinks of stupid things during a fire. But garden hose drinking was now part of his loops routine. At least he wasn't thirsty.

As he kept looping my neighbor's house across the street and to the left was engulfed now. All the homes across the street on fire. He looked over the fence at his next-door neighbor. Her house was still standing, but her yard was decorated with wood chips... which were now on fire. A low fire, not a fearsome fire, but burning towards Eric's wooden fence. The gate was open, creating a firebreak, but he couldn't chance it. He had to put the fire out in her yard. And, again, his garden hose wasn't long enough. He ran out to the street and over to the front of her fence and got in through the gate. He ran looking for her garden hoses, but he had left his flashlight behind. It was so dark that he could not find her spigots or her garden hoses. Eric ran back and on the way across her yards, caught his foot on some unseen landscaping border and went down hard. In the dark, he never saw the metal edging along her walkway. He wasn't hurt and adrenaline had him going. He got up and ran home, grabbed the flashlight, and returned. He found her spigots and her garden hoses and got the water running. He put out the fire in her backyard wood chips. Her fence was on fire too; burning towards her house. He put out her fence. *Gee, wouldn't it be great if I saved two homes?*

He hustled back to my house to keep doing loops.

One thing about this fire is that the usual resources we've come to rely upon, to help us were overwhelmed and simply not there. He kept having that thought that at some point, some fire truck crew would show up and help him. This is how the world works. We get into trouble, we struggle to get out of trouble, then help arrives and saves us. With every siren going up The Ridgway, he had held on to that hope. They were only a block away.

Why couldn't they come down this street to help me? I've been working so hard to save my home, to save the life I've known. I deserve a break.

He'd gone into his backyard and was putting out a spot fire when all of a sudden, a car horn blasted!

Someone was honking a car horn! They'd come down my street and probably seen my Subaru running with the lights on and knew someone was back here! They were honking to check for me! My first break. He dropped the hose and ran to the front.

He did not want them to miss him. *They would help the guy that was here all by himself if they saw me. Who wouldn't?* Eric was an epic underdog. People love the underdog.

He got to the front and saw no cars in the street, except his Subaru, running with the lights on. Across the street in a neighbor's side yard, a pickup truck was on fire. The cab was burning. It had shorted the horn. That was the car horn he'd heard. At that point, it felt like the wind had been taken from his sails. It was becoming obvious. There would be no help. The safety net was gone. He had been a fool to hope for a rescue. He had just gone from the highest of highs to a punch in the gut. It was him against the fire. It always had been and until the end, it would be. No miracles were going to happen.

He went back to his loops.

Thursday 9:47am - Genna, ID

Holly and Phillis joined a crowd of about twenty-five and counting, many of whom were exhibiting various signs of grief and fear, in the Walgreens parking lot. Three Genna Police officers were trying to calm them. They handed each of them a paper face mask, not that they thought it would help with this acrid smoke. Holly really wished there were goggles, her eyes were watering nonstop. As she looked around, she could see that some commercial buildings were surviving so far, not all, but some. It seemed big parking lots helped, as there were no burning trees surrounding them. There were, of course, tons of flying embers, she was certain that those had caused fires that had burned several of the buildings, despite the big parking lot. She had only seen one restaurant that had survived so far, but admittedly she had been sidetracked during her walk down the Ridgway, keeping Phyllis moving... and upright.

Fire surrounded them, but Walgreens was currently a mini-oasis. The hillside behind them raged, the neighborhood next to them was burning too. Everything across the street from them seemed to be aflame. Here, so far so good.

A blonde female officer, Officer Natalie Horne, addressed the growing crowd, "Folks, please stay together. We have two busses on the way up and we expect this crowd to grow."

"How long is it going to be?"

"How will the bus get through the traffic?"

"What if the wind shifts?"

The crowd peppered her with questions. They were stuck in the eye of an inferno, who could blame them. They were anxious. The GPD officers had now run out of face masks to hand out. Some were coughing, others had given their masks to older people that had joined the group.

"That is all the information that I have, at the moment, but they are on the way, and I promise you that I will give you every update that I get. When I know, you'll know. Trust me, we don't want to be here anymore than you do."

Natalie had only been a police officer for eight months. She was hired straight out of the academy by the Genna PD. But she was still handling herself with tremendous poise and her calm confidence eased the crowd's anxiety a bit. She had always had a strength about her that people trusted. Of course, it shouldn't have surprised anyone. She was, after all the daughter of Sheriff Ezra Horne. Many thought that he had arranged the position in Genna for her, partly because it was a relatively sleepy town with little violent crime. But the truth was, Ezra wasn't the type to coddle, even if it meant she was a bit safer. Natalie earned her way here. She wouldn't have accepted the position, had she thought her father was trying to do such a thing, she was much too independent for that.

A crash came from the burning building next to them, as the diner's sign came down onto a nearby telephone pole. The pole did not contain the impact well and moments later it too crashed down, into the adjacent parking lot, bringing power and phone lines down with it. Sparks flew as the down cable hit the ground.

Natalie thumbed her mic, "Dispatch, I was told power was shut down, town-wide. But I have a downed power pole here sparking everywhere. It sure seems to be live to me. Valley Rd and Ridgway. Southeast corner."

"Copy, downed pole. Hold a minute while I contact Idaho electric."

"Roger that."

She looked around the parking lot, there were a number of other poles that potentially threatened the crowd that had by now grown to around eighty. Decisively, she walked over to the front door of the Walgreens. When it didn't open, she pounded the door. She knew one of the managers was in the building. She had seen him watching the chaos through the store's front windows a few times. He emerged from an office on the side of the building and peeked around an endcap to see who was knocking. She waved him over, observed the sigh and slight hesitation before making his way to the front door.

"Can I help you, Officer?" He shouted from inside the still-closed doors.

"Yes, you can start by opening the door so we can talk."

"It's against protocol to open the doors when the power is out and all customers have left the store."

That raised her shackles. "Sir, open the door, right now."

"It's not my decision. I would have to call the manager first."

"That's going to be kind of difficult since the whole town is on fire. Open the door, right now. Last chance."

By now she had attracted the attention of the other two officers. She waved one of them over, indicating to the other to stay with the crowd of... refugees, was the only word that came to mind. The first officer jogged to her side.

"I think we need to get these people inside for safety, in case more power lines come down, but this guy won't open the door to even discuss it. He's giving off a real nervous vibe too."

Officer Matthews pulled the large Maglite

flashlight from his belt and rapped three times loudly as he stared the man in the face, mouthing the word 'NOW' as he did.

The man blanched a bit before coming to acceptance. He walked up and turned the deadbolt. The instant he did, Natalie yanked the door open, ripping it from his hands.

"I was going to ask nicely. But now you are going to do exactly what I say without question. Do you understand?"

The man looked at Officer Matthews, pleadingly. "Sir, I tried to tell her it is against policy..."

Matthews grabbed him by the front of the shirt and dragged him outside. "All of those people need shelter. Power lines are coming down around us, so don't talk to me about policy." He yelled to his partner, "Dave, bring them into the store."

"You can't do that."

"I just did. You should have cooperated with Officer Horne. Then we wouldn't be having this little problem."

They left the door propped open and went back inside. Natalie was nowhere in sight. Matthews and his partner Officer Rivera guided the group into the entryway of the store. As Matthews helped get folks settled, most were sitting on the floor, some preferred to stand, he kept a close eye on the 'manager' whose name he had learned was Robert. He was clearly uncomfortable and kept glancing back toward the offices. His earpiece chirped and he heard a voice whisper.

"Danny, grab your new friend by the back of his collar and drag him back to the pharmacy. Do not let him walk out that door."

Matthews looked up at Robert and could see outright fear. He kept one hand pressed to his ear and pretended to talk as he paced back towards the door, to cut off any potential escape route. He hoped that Robert would connect the dots about the cell towers being down. "Will do. See you soon."

Robert made his move to cut and run, but quick thinking by Matthews gave him the few steps and the proper angle to cut him off in time. And he did, with a menacing straight-arm that threw Robert off balance and used his momentum against him as he slammed into the door frame, hard. The officer was on him in an instant and felt all the fight drain out of him.

Robert knew he was done for. It would have been so easy, too. That bitch ruined it all. Matthews hauled him to his feet, dragged him over to the cosmetics counter, away from most of the 'refugees' and forced his face down onto the counter before expertly cuffing him. With a slight extra squeeze, he closed the cuffs an extra notch, making them nice and tight, for being dumb enough to make a run for it. Though Robert complained, he didn't realize how much more it would have hurt if he had made Matthews actually chase him down.

"Hey Dave, I'll be in the pharmacy. Once everyone is settled, go stand out front in case you find any more stragglers."

Dave nodded. Matthews stood Robert up and marched him back towards the pharmacy. Natalie waited at the door.

"What's your name again?" She asked the handcuffed man.

"Robert Machado."

"Robert, we have a few things that need to be explained. What's your title here?"

"I am an Assistant Manager."

"So, Mr. Assistant Manager Robert Machado, care to explain why, in the middle of an absolutely horrific disaster, there is a duffle bag in here stuffed with every Vicodin, Percocet, Oxy, Fentanyl, morphine, and Dilaudid bottle in the store?"

"I was doing inventory, so we could make an accurate claim after this was over. You know, in case the store burns."

She laughed. "Out of all the merchandise in this store, it is interesting that you are only inventorying the pain killers. I am assuming that is the same excuse you are going to give me for the open safe in the office and the half-filled, matching duffle bag of cash on the floor in there."

Robert blanched and was staring at his shoes by now. Matthews yanked down on the back of his collar, which forced his head up. "What was the plan, Robert? To wait it out in here until the town was deserted and just drive away with the loot? Do you realize nearly the entire town is on fire? Why did you possibly think you could survive here when everything else is burning."

"We have sprinklers," he mumbled.

Dave and Natalie looked at each other and laughed. Natalie jumped in, "Hey genius, the town's water supply is screwed up because of the fire. Even the fire hydrants have no water. Sprinklers are only as good as the water supply allows them to be. You would have burnt in here with your new-found stash, you moron."

"Let's get him back up to the front and secure him to something. We have bigger issues to deal with than this idiot. If we live through this, he is going down."

10:04am- Genna, ID

James was exhausted. It was early in the day, though the darkness suggested otherwise. It had been quite an ordeal. Kylie and the kids had hitched a ride down the hill with the water tanker as it went to refill, there was no more water to be had up on the hill. He had seen them off with hugs and well-wishes, before beginning to walk down Ridgway himself. Traffic was barely moving, so walking seemed like a better idea. Everything along both sides the street seemed to be burning. His mind flashed back to his college days, reading Dante's Inferno and he briefly wondered which level of hell this was. He passed actively burning buildings, smoldering ruins, and burnt-out cars, along with what seemed to be hundreds of cars and trucks filled with families, pets and whatever belongings could be shoved in around them. Each carload hoping that they wouldn't be the next burning hull along the side of the road. The smoke was bad but seemed to mostly linger about ten to twelve feet off the ground, making him feel like he wasn't yet killing himself from smoke inhalation, though Tristan had given him a few minutes of pure oxygen after the cemetery ordeal. That had cleared his head. He didn't know what else he could do to help. He said a silent prayer of thanks for having made it out with those kids. To this point, at least.

Tristan and the fire guys, being out of water, had

offered him a ride, but it seemed to him that he would be able to walk faster than traffic would go. Besides, he wasn't terribly eager to get back into an enclosed vehicle after practically being baked in his own. He was nearly downtown anyway, and just beyond downtown was the route down to Rome. Thank God, it's a downhill walk.

He walked between the lanes of cars to give himself a buffer from the heat of the fires on each side. It didn't help much, but it sure beat being on what passed for sidewalks in a mountain town. Soon, he realized that he was close to home, or what presumably used to be home. He had to accept the fact that it was likely gone. But now wasn't the time to dwell on it. At the next intersection, where he would normally turn to go home, was the infamous Ridgway bottleneck. Six years ago, the then Town Council, which included the current Mayor, Joanna Moody, had decided that the downtown business district needed more storefront parking. In order to accomplish that they had removed a lane of traffic each direction, changing four lanes into two, through downtown before opening up again. Despite, an uproar from the residents, the situation remained. And James could see now, the cost of such a decision. People would die because of it.

At the intersection, he saw Josh Florini, whose office was only a few buildings down from the intersection. He was wearing shorts and an orange vest as he and a GPD officer tried in vain to direct traffic and keep the flow moving. It didn't seem to be working. Drivers were scared and impatient, for good reason, but by overreacting and trying to break through, they were really only destroying any chance for a steady flow of traffic. Trying to get more than twenty-five thousand people off a hill, in a matter of a couple of hours, was an impossible task, especially with only two of the four evacuation routes opened. Well, technically Pulga Road had reopened once the hospital finished evacuating, but it was inaccessible for most of the town. He sauntered over to where Josh was standing with his back to him.

"Hey Josh, how's your day been? I was on my way to your office first thing this morning, but I seem to have gotten sidetracked." He tried to keep things light.

Josh turned and looked at the smoke and soot-covered voice. "It looks like you've had fun. Us too. This bottleneck worked exactly as we predicted for all these years. This is insane."

"Wife and kids get out okay?"

"Yeah, I sent them out right away. Though, with no cell, I have no idea where they are. But I am sure they are in Rome somewhere waiting to hear from me."

"Okay, good. What can I do to help?"

"Do you mind being in the line of fire?" He looked around at the flames, then at James' charred and soot-covered clothes and chuckled before adding, "Figuratively, speaking of course."

"I am pretty certain that I don't have a choice."

Josh called out to the GPD officer standing across the intersection, "Hey Joey, do you have any more yellow vests in your squad car?"

Officer Thompson motioned for the cars stopped in front of him to stay put and went over to his car, parked on the sidewalk at the intersect with lights flashing. He popped the trunk and grabbed a vest and a bottle of water from an ice chest and delivered them both to James.

James hadn't even realized how thirsty he was, but he swigged half the bottle of water before thinking that he should probably take it easy. He put the vest on and walked to the downhill side of the intersection and stood on the double yellow lines in the middle of the street. Both lanes were being utilized to get folks down the hill, making it essentially a one-way street. But people kept trying to hurry and create a third 'middle' lane which was part of what was slowing things down, because once they got to the end of downtown they were forced to merge back into two lanes to get past the concrete barriers at the intersection before crossing the intersection and opening up into four lanes again. He was to be the barrier in the center that forced them into one of the two lanes and, with luck, improve the flow of traffic. He just hoped that people didn't get impatient enough to simply run him over.

As he took in the four corners, it was good to see that the flags were still waving and the Veteran's Hall was still standing as it was surrounded by grass and a good size parking lot, it had fewer trees to spread fire to it. Across the street, James' favorite pizza place still stood too. The other two corners hadn't fared so well, as the auto shop and a gas station were both virtually gone.

James guided cars that had been waved through, by either Josh or Officer Thompson, into one of the two 'proper' lanes and within fifteen or twenty minutes (time seemed to have different rules today), as the triple lane of cars cleared the intersection at the other end of downtown, traffic did actually begin to flow. Not quickly, but at least constantly in motion which was a huge improvement from the logjam that it had been.

Thursday 10:10am - Genna, ID

It was a solitary battle, but Eric was winning it one spot fire at a time. His home was the only home that he could see that wasn't burning. His continuous circuits were exhausting, but he had been able to put at least twenty spot fires out in the last hour or so. It was hot and smoky, but he was winning.

Eric came around the right side from the back to the front yard, another spot fire was burning a bush on the other side of the house. He quickly grabbed the front hose nozzle and dragged the hose over that direction, then pulled the trigger and starting spraying the bush. After a few seconds of spray, something changed. The water pressure dropped, then it dropped more. He tried squeezing the nozzle's trigger harder, but within seconds it was at such a slow drizzle that it didn't even spray, but dribbled down his hand. He looked back along the length of the hose toward the spigot, to see where the kink was. He couldn't see one. Eric dropped the nozzle and hustled back along the length of the hose, physically tracing its path; still no kink. He ran around the other side of the house and across the back yard to the back hose nearest the fire. He picked that one up... he got one quick burst of water as the hose released the built-up pressure, then it too faded into mere drops.

He was hit by the realization that it was over. The battle lost. Here he was, a solitary figure, fighting a massive fire all morning armed with three hoses and a flashlight, and now the hoses were out of the equation.

To be thorough, or maybe out of desperation, he went over to his last remaining hose and pulled the trigger. Same story, pressure release, then nothing. He felt his spirit release in much the same way as all the fight left his consciousness. He too deflated. Out of options, he walked back around the other side and out to the front and stood in the middle of the front yard. He watched the burning bush, fueled by the wind get bigger and soon the next bush was burning too. One by one, the heat continued to dry and preheat the bush next to them, then ignite. He watched, entranced by the horrific beauty of the flame's movement. A larger bush went up, right on the corner of the house, Eric watched as it grew more intense before, pulling oxygen from ground level, it began to climb and swirl as it grew taller. It licked the underside of the eaves that served as the roof's overhang. Ignition wasn't the slow 'smolder, then burn' process like in a fireplace. It was more like a molecular level explosion as the dried-out cells of the wood that composed the eave all accepted the flame and absorbed it like a thirsty sponge. Within seconds, the whole corner of the house, eaves, and roof alike was burning. Soon smoke was pouring out the roof's exhaust vent.

Eric watched his house slowly become engulfed, one section at a time. He wasn't horrified, or even terribly sad. This was the inevitable conclusion. This was the reason that he had defied his wife and stayed to fight it. Yes, the house was burning. But in his heart, he had done everything within his power to prevent it. That was his closure, knowing that there was nothing else he could have done. He had given his all and could look back without regret.

Now, it was time for Eric and his flashlight to get in the car and drive away.

Thursday 10:22 am - North of Rome, ID

Jillian drove down the hill and finally found a cell. She had stopped by her office at Town Hall and gathered up her computer tower and as many of the servers as she could get to and loaded them into her car. She hadn't known how to power the servers down properly, but she hoped they would be okay anyway. Regardless, they had a better chance of working now, than if she had left them to burn. Ultimately the government would have to find a way to govern, even amidst this fiasco.

Finally, her phone connected. "Jilli, is that you? Are you okay?" Joanna's voice blared over the car's speakers.

"I just got down the hill. Are you and Don, okay?"

"Ummm," she hesitated, "yes, we stayed in Rome last night anyway. Is it bad?"

The nerve of this woman. 'Is it bad?' Of course, it is freaking bad. The whole town is on fire. If she wasn't such a useful tool, Jillian would have kicked her to the curb years ago. Now, unfortunately, she needed the Mayor.

"Reach out to all the other Council-members and make sure they evac'd safely. We'll need to get on top of this pronto, have you spoken to the Sheriff?"

"No, why?"

"Why? Because he is the top law enforcement officer in the county. Because he called a mandatory evacuation for the entire town of Genna, of which, you are the Mayor. It never occurred to you that maybe you should reach out to his office and stay updated on the situation?"

"Why are you getting so huffy with me? I just found out about the fire thirty minutes ago, when I took my coffee out on the back porch and saw the smoke. I will call Ezra's office after I eat breakfast."

Jillian was about to lose her cool, but with today's nightmare, she knew that she needed to reign it in, "Okay, I have to go. Update me if you find any news from the Sheriff

Thursday 11:27 am - Rome, ID

Michael followed his wife and mother-in-law to the mall, located only a few short blocks from Costco. Traffic was really heavy, even for Rome's standards. Few semi-rural towns could absorb twenty thousand people, especially distraught and distracted drivers, driving cars stuffed with likely everything that they now owned. Once he got them settled, he said his farewells and took off, in search of answers. He drove back over to 'the bottom' of the hill, the shopping center located on The Ridgway, just as it was entering Rome. There was a WinCo supermarket, a Starbucks and all of the typical nail salons and Thai restaurants that tend to pepper these types of shopping strips; including a mattress store. He could see another one across the street.

Why does there seem to be a mattress store on every corner? How often does one buy a bed?

Of course, looking at the volcano-like mountain above, he suspected that a great many would be needing beds now. Most importantly, in Michael's estimation at the moment, the shopping center had a huge parking lot with an unobstructed view up the mountain. Well, unobstructed aside from the muddied smoke top hat that seemed to rest on the ridge's peak. What had initially been a large black column of smoke was now starting to spread out across the area. Michael had seen a number of people wearing masks already, although it didn't seem that much smoke had settled down into Rome...yet.

He had already stopped near the roadblock and tried to get info from the State Trooper manning the barricade, but he hadn't yet been up to the hill. He had simply been ordered to close the upward lanes. He had nothing to offer Michael. The Starbucks looked to be packed, maybe he could find someone with answers in there. He drove around until he found a place to park.

He decided that he better deal with finding a place to stay before he went in. He pulled up a list of local hotels on his phone. Five phone calls later, he was feeling some anxiety. There was nothing available. There were only a few hotels and motels in Rome. He had called them all, even the ones he would never have wanted to stay at under any other circumstance. He tried the casino about thirty minutes away. No vacancy.

Chapter Six

Thursday Noon - Bear County, ID

Joshua Florini gave James a ride out of town, once the Ridgway traffic had eased up a bit. They had both seen enough and done enough for one day. It was surreal. They were both fairly animated people, though Josh was the more serious one, neither had much to say. It was as if neither of them had had a chance to think about it, they had simply sprung into action, now that they were descending off the ridge, somehow the enormity of it hit home. They rode in near silence for about ten minutes before James broke the ice.

"Well, something tells me that y'all aren't going to need that new sewer system, now. Huh?"

"Joanna's pipe dream, pun intended, was never going to happen anyway," Josh replied without tearing his eyes from the road.

"What, I thought it was a done deal. Starting next month. No?"

"You know as much about this town as anybody, James. Did you really fall for Joanna's campaign nonsense?" Josh shook his head.

"Oh my God. She hasn't got Council approval, does she? She hasn't even told you." James asked.

"James, I don't know what you are babbling about, but I assure you there is no hope for the sewer, especially now. You've been to the Council meetings; you know that they would have been shouting from the rooftops if we had approved that mess."

"No, no, no. You aren't hearing me. Jillian paid me a surprise visit the morning after the election..." He paused for a second to reflect, "God, was that only yesterday? It feels like a lifetime ago, now. Anyway, after my AA meeting on Wednesday morning, I walked out and Jillian was leaning against my trunk, waiting for me."

"What did she want, to gloat?" Josh interrupted.

Their attention was suddenly deflected, as they passed a section where the fire had come up out of the Salmon River Canyon and was burning its way toward the lone neighborhood that stood in between Genna and Rome. It was a relatively new development with mostly four hundred to six hundred-thousand-dollar homes. That was a lot for these parts.

"Good God, the fire is all the way down here. Do you have any cell, yet?" Josh asked.

James checked his phone, he had one bar. "We are close, I have one bar, the first that I have had all day. Keep going, maybe it'll get better in a minute or two, then we can call this in."

Another half mile down the road the cell showed a second, quickly followed by a third bar and data service returned. He dialed 911, but only got a busy signal in response. He redialed, got the same signal. The third and fourth tries came back with the same result. "Crap, the lines are overloaded."

Josh pulled his phone out and hit a speed dial number. It was answered on the second ring. "Sheriff's Office, this is Maggie."

"Hey Maggie, It's Josh Florini." Maggie worked as a secretary in the Sheriff's office in Rome. She and Josh's wife, Stephanie had been friends for nearly a decade.

"Oh my gosh, Josh. Are you okay? And the family?"

"I am okay, my family got out as soon as I heard news of the fire, so they should be fine. Anyway, 911 is crashed. Do you know if they have evacuated Centerville? We've had no cell on the Ridge since early morning. The fire is burning pretty heavily down in Salmon River Canyon."

"I haven't heard anything about that! I will double-check though. Give me a second." Her voice was replaced by the sound of keys clicking rapidly, "We did get a call from an elderly man claiming that he couldn't drive and needed to get out of Centerville, but it didn't mention a fire. He was told we didn't have any resources available at that time. I think they thought he was just looking for a ride. You sure the fire is headed that way?"

"No, but this thing moves so fast, I would evacuate anyone in that entire canyon because I know it is burning down as far as The Precipice sub-division."

"Okay, let me get this called out. Be safe Josh, glad you're okay."

Josh looked ahead to see exactly where they were. "Wait, Maggie. Do you have an address for the old guy that needed a ride? I'm pretty close to there."

"Ummm... The guy's name is Walter; the address is 254 Honey Run, just off of Salmon Run Rd."

"Okay, we'll do a drive-by and see what the status is. Thanks, Maggie."

They were only a mile from the turnoff to Salmon Run Rd. He slowed and got into the right lane. The smoke was much lighter here, it almost looked like daytime. Once they turned the road went winding through the foothills, it took them past the old wooden covered bridge over Old Butte Creek. The historic landmark was built in 1886 and is the only surviving example of a three-span timber Pratt-type bridge in the United States. Originally built as an uncovered bridge, the roof was added in 1901. The beautifully picturesque spot was a popular location for weddings and family photoshoots.

They wound around for another half mile until they came out into the actual Salmon River Canyon. They could see the flames covering the eastern banks all the way up to the rim of the canyon... to Genna and beyond. Though it was still a mile away, they could see the wind spreading embers and ash throughout the valley. The sky here looked more dirty brown than the blacks and grays that Genna had had this morning.

Josh took the next left onto Honey Run and wound his way up to the address that Maggie had given them. They found the number and pulled into the dirt and gravel driveway. In front of them was a nice piece of property scattered with old oak trees creating an abundance of shade. The house was a double-wide mobile home, that appeared to have once been pretty nice, but clearly, it had been neglected for a number of years. The steps to the front porch deck were rotted and covered in intricate spider webs. On the carport side, they could see a ramp leading up to the deck from the side. Josh and

James chose to approach via the ramp and knocked on the door. They gave it a minute, then knocked again. With no answer, they turned to head back down the ramp but were greeted by the readily identifiable sound of a shotgun being racked as the slide pushed a cartridge into the chamber. Before them sat a man, in his mid-seventies with disheveled hair and clothes that looked like he had been working on a farm, in a wheelchair.

"I don't take you two for looters, and even the Mormons and Jehovah's Witness folks wouldn't be out here with Armageddon coming. So, what do ya want?"

James spoke first, "You must be Walter. A friend at the Sheriff's office told us you might need a ride. I'm James, and this here's Joshua Florini. He's on the Town Council up in Genna." He reached his hand out to shake but was met with the unfriendly end of a shotgun barrel.

The old man's eyes glanced over at the top of the canyon, then settled on Josh, "Looks to me like you're going to need a new job. Ain't nothin' left of Genna far as I can tell."

Josh was about to correct him, that he had a real job, the Council was primarily community service and only paid about three hundred dollars per month. But then decided that arguing with a shotgun aimed at your face was a bad idea.

"I suppose that's one possibility. We just came from there, it isn't good."

"Hell son, Armageddon ain't supposed to be fun."

James smiled; despite the shotgun, he liked the old coot. Josh seemed much less certain.

"Great, I got a few duffel bags packed up out by the greenhouse. Gotta take my medicine and stuff. If you boys would grab those for me, then we can get goin' before it gets worse here." With that, he laid the shotgun across his lap and spun the wheelchair around headed down the ramp. He pointed around the side of the mobile home to the rear. "They're right over there."

James and Josh hustled around the corner and found the makeshift greenhouse. The door was propped open by four enormous military-style duffels. They quickly grabbed them and headed around to the front, but Walter was nowhere in sight. They trudged the heavy bags over to Josh's SUV only to find Walter buckled happily into the front passenger seat. Josh gave James a look and a slight shoulder shrug. James just shook his head.

They popped the hatch and loaded it, barely, into the rear compartment. James walked around to the passenger side and opened to door to get in the back seat. But Walter's wheelchair had been folded and unceremoniously shoved into the backseat, scratching the black leather along the way. "If you can't walk, how did you get this in here? An where am I supposed to sit?"

"Who says I can't walk?"

"You're in a wheelchair and have a ramp going up to the house."

"I'm not in a wheelchair, now am I?" with a finality that let James know the conversation was over.

A sudden gust of wind ripped the door handle from James's hand so hard that it actually bent the hinge as it overextended. A shower of red-hot embers flew over them riding the wind to their next destination. He tried to cover himself with his hands. Out of the corner of his eye, he saw Josh jump into the front seat and close the door. James quickly stepped to the front side of the door to push the door closed against the strong wind, it didn't budge. He gave it a quick short burst of strength and heard the fatigued hinge pop, before releasing and allow James to only fight the wind. He slammed the door, then ran around to the other side and opened that door, he made sure to keep a sure grip on the door handle this time. He leapt in, taking a wheelchair handle in the ribs as he did so, and pulled it closed. It was raining ash and embers, though he didn't see anything in the immediate vicinity catch fire.

"Time to go Josh."

"Yep."

Walter chimed in, "This is a pretty nice Toyota, but you gotta get that back door looked at. It's popping and making all kinds of weird noises."

Josh sighed, "It's a Lexus."

"Yeah, you ever been to Japan? In Japan, Lexus means 'Toyota that Americans pay too much for'." He laughed. James smiled. Josh started driving.

They wound back out of the canyon, pausing only to look at the one hundred thirty-two-year-old covered bridge, now burning above Old Butte Creek. James tried to take a picture of the historic structure, but his phone was dead.

As they turned back out onto The Ridgway toward Rome, "Walter, where would you like me to take you? Do you have someplace to go?"

"Well, my ex-wife lives on the Northside of Rome, so I ain't going that way. But I got me a lady friend that lives in the apartments right near the bottom of the hill, off Forest."

It was then that Josh noticed a powerful odor, pungent, yet sweet. To overpower the smell of smoke-infused in his hair, clothes, and nostrils it must be really strong, what the hell was it? Then it dawned on him.

"Walter was there anything in your bags besides

your medicine. Clothes, keepsakes… anything?"

"Nope, I told you I had to bring my medicine."

James laughed out loud, "You conned a sitting Town Council member to transport marijuana during a disaster? That's classic." He guffawed.

"Ain't no con, it is my medicine. I am nothing if not honest."

"What would you have done if the actual Sheriff's Deputies that you called had shown up?"

"Same thing. They have trunks, they wouldn't notice." He looked at Josh, "Ain't my fault your Toyota don't have a trunk."

Thursday 12:15 pm - Council, ID

It took DJ nearly two and a half hours to make the drive out of Genna and back to their motel. There were times when he seriously doubted that they would make it out, but most of the time had been spent sitting, idling in traffic with everyone else. There were also times that he felt like dropping Bud off a cliff on the way back.

They had gone up to Genna early in the morning but never imagined being trapped by the fire. They were both dressed in black and each wore the logo of RomaSol, a local solar company, on their breast pocket. They were door-knocking a couple of specific neighborhoods trying to talk to homeowners and gather information. They had only made it to two houses when all hell broke loose. The fire crashed over the lip of the canyon, like a wave. Bud had been at the back of a house overlooking the canyon when it happened; his right pant-leg catching fire, along with his right arm. DJ had been inside, dealing with the homeowner when he heard the scream. He had just reached the back door when he saw a ball of flame run from the back patio towards the stables and leap into a large galvanized steel water trough. He finished up what he was doing, before locking the front door and pulling it closed behind him. He rushed around to the stables to check on his partner. Flames had now taken hold of the trees along the edge of the property and had spread to the roof of the main house. The horses were clearly agitated and were being quite vocal in their distress. He felt a twinge of guilt that he couldn't help them. He couldn't tell how many there were but there were certainly several.

DJ helped Bud get out of the trough and helped him get out to the car on the street. Fire trucks were just arriving. He dragged Bud the rest of the way and threw him across the back seat, then ran around and jumped in behind the wheel. He took off, without really knowing which way to go, but he knew he wanted to be gone before any of the first responders noticed them.

That is what led him to want to throw Bud off a cliff; the incessant moaning and sobbing made it difficult for DJ to concentrate on what was a very difficult drive out of town. Sure, he had a pretty bad burn, but EJ had seen worse. Hell, he'd had worse. He didn't moan about it like a baby. He was a man about it.

DJ helped Bud to their room in the motel. As soon as the door banged shut behind them, Bud fell onto the closest of two double beds. The carpet was frayed and there was a subtle unidentifiable odor that had plagued DJ's sense of smell since they had arrived three days ago. But now, his only olfactory perception was the smell of smoke.

He turned to Bud. "Look, you need to man up! I'll run down to the drugstore and get something for you, but if you moan and cry as you did in the car someone will notice us. The idea is for us to be invisible. So keep your trap shut until I get back. Then we have to call the boss."

Bud didn't respond, he simply laid back a let out a small whimper. "I'll be back soon. Don't answer the door for anybody, got it?"

Moments later, he was driving down Main Street which was a section the Old US Highway 95. He didn't need directions; the town of Council only covered a little over one and a half square miles. There were only about one thousand residents here, but many more came into town from the surrounding county to shop and get necessities. Theirs was the only motel in the area, but it was quiet and out of the way. There was a drugstore just up the road. He stopped and picked up bandages, burn ointment and ibuprofen, as well as a case of water before heading back. DJ drove slow and easy, careful not to attract any unwanted attention in this sleepy town. Traffic had increased a bit from what it had been over the last couple of days. When he reached the motel, DJ was surprised to see the parking lot full. His had been one of only three cars in the lot when he left only moments ago. He realized that the evacuees were arriving en masse now. They were going to need to be much more careful now, but perhaps blending in with the crowd would be easier than avoiding it.

He found a parking spot, next to a minivan with the plastic lenses of its taillights melted and drooping down to the rear bumper, and made his way into their room. Bud was asleep. Dj took notice of the three, now empty, mini liquor bottles on the nightstand, and shook his head. Bud had raided the mini-fridge, which further disturbed DJ because they still had a job to do, injured or not.

DJ woke his perturbed partner and cleaned and wrapped the burns on his arm. Bud groaned loudly as he wrapped it. DJ had had enough, "Listen to me, you idiot. The hotel is now overloaded with other guests. Keep your whining to yourself. You can wrap your leg, yourself, but you best be ready to get back to work tonight, we have a job to do!" DJ threw the bottle of ibuprofen to him and walked out, "I have to find a quiet place to go call the boss. He's not going to be happy."

DJ left and drove just a block down the road and pulled into the parking lot for a mid-sized grocery store. He parked well away from the other cars and sat facing the street. He pulled out the phone, a burner with only one number programmed into it, and pressed a button. It was answered on the first ring.

"What is your status?" the voice said.

"We are back at the motel now. Bud was slightly injured, but should be fine."

"No names over an open line you idiot. Has he become a liability?"

"No, he'll be fine... or I will ensure that he isn't a liability."

"What's the status of your assignment?"

"Hell, boss, we barely got started before the fire breached the canyon rim, right into our face. We had only made two stops on the list, I thought we would have more time. But it should be fine they all burned anyway."

"Have you confirmed this?"

"Confirmed what?"

"That all the places on your list burned."

"Well, no, but... The whole damn town burned, it was like nothing that I have ever seen."

"Then choose your words more carefully. If you haven't physically confirmed it, don't tell me that they all fucking burned. What of the two visits that you made?"

"Yes, sir. They went as expected. They didn't want to sign, but we had a rather quick negotiation and found, umm, resolution."

"Okay, so your original assignment is now on hold. You will get up there and verify the destruction of the other forty-seven properties."

"They have the town locked down now, we'll never get in."

"You best get creative. I chose you because you have a reputation for thinking outside the box and getting the job done. Though I must say that this conversation raises some doubt."

"Yes, sir."

"I want results, you have forty-eight hours. Get moving."

Thursday 12:30pm - Rome, ID

The Bear County Fairgrounds bustled with activity; men and women scrambled around trying to get the new command center set up. Dozens of fire trucks from around the State and from eastern portions of Oregon and Washington had arrived. Several crews had been sent up the hill to help, but the reality was they had been sent up blind. The command center simply had virtually no verifiable situational information to work with yet. Chief Joey Oliver had taken command of getting the base of operations set up. Though he had no actual authority to take command, he had the access and equipment to get this going and he would run with it until somebody figured out who was in charge. He knew that until they had communications and satellite links set up, they had no situational control. Now that he had arrived in Rome, it was obvious that this was an even more dangerous situation than it had seemed from the NICC in Boise. Forty-mile an hour winds, with gusts over sixty-five miles an hour, made this an incredibly fast-moving and a terribly unpredictable fire.

He had rallied the 'outside' teams to the fairgrounds as soon as he had rolled in. Many had shown up almost immediately, as they had already arrived from their individual posts, which was great. But now he had a bunch of teams twiddling their thumbs while waiting for orders. Until the tech guys got him up and running, he had no idea how things had changed over the last two hours on the ground. Therefore, he had no plan.

They were setting up in two of the expo buildings on the fairground's property; both buildings were identical and ran parallel to each other, each running nearly one hundred yards in length and twenty yards wide. They resembled old beige brick arch-top airplane hangars with giant barn doors on either end and several normal doors opening outward along each side. Movable partitions divided the interior space into meeting-sized rooms, though they had all been removed from building #1 where Joey was standing. This would be the Command Center. Generators outside were tethered to the central computing hub by thick snakes of heavy gauge wire. At the far end of the tunnel-like building, a couple of people were setting up chairs while an AV guy set up a whiteboard and a podium for a makeshift briefing room. Along one wall were several large print maps of the region with various blowups of specific areas, the largest one was of the Town of Genna.

"How are we coming, David?" Joey asked the tech nearest him.

"If everything goes right, we should have you up and running in ten to fifteen minutes… so you better plan for twenty. That's the reality. Going as fast as we can."

"I'll leave you to it then." He turned back toward what he considered the front of the building. There were a few people setting up long tables, along the walls just inside the barn door, with tubs of ice and bottled water.

Joey was about to turn away when he noticed a new guy walk in wearing soot-stained Nomex pants and a long-sleeve tee-shirt that was drenched in sweat. The sweat induced soot streaks on his face were reminiscent of an 'after-the-show' pic of Alice Cooper's makeup job. This guy wasn't a performer. He stopped to grab a water bottle, drank half of it, then wiped his mouth with the back of his hand smearing even more black across the lower half of his face. He looked around and made eye contact with Joey, and walked over.

"You in charge here?"

"I suppose I am, for the moment, don't know who's supposed to take command on this fire, but I am getting the base set up so we're ready." He put his hand out in introduction, "Joey Oliver."

"Tristan Byrne. Glad to meet you, Chief. What's going on here chief? You've got thirty plus companies hanging out in the parking lot while people are dying up on the ridge. What gives?"

"We just arrived and are getting set up.

Honestly, we don't have enough current situational details to create a plan, yet. Another couple of hundred companies are en route, should be arriving over the next hour. Is it as bad as it looks?"

Tristan let out a deep breath, his eyes threatened to tear up for the first time. His voice quivered, "It's gone."

"What's gone?"

"Genna is gone. Obviously, I didn't have time to count buildings for the bean counters, but I would put it at ninety to ninety-five percent gone. Total shitshow, we were never even in a position to fight it before it jumped us and continued on its way. Faster and hotter than anything I have ever seen. Hell, at one point there was a firenado moving through the center of town. Total insanity. The last hour or more, we simply sat along the evac routes and tried to keep flames off the lines of traffic, trying to get out. Frankly, we even failed at that to some extent. Especially after the hydrants went dry. Once our tanks were dry, we came down the hill."

"Wait, a real firenado in town? You saw this?" Joey's inner science geek climbed to the forefront of his consciousness.

"I watched it develop not thirty yards from me. Terrifyingly beautiful. I had only ever seen videos of them created in labs, I honestly didn't think they existed in nature. But there it was taking out parked cars and almost took out a Rite Aid."

"Okay, when this is all over, I want to talk to you more about this. I teach Fire Science at the NIFC. Few people have seen them, I'd like to talk to you more."

"Have you seen Captain Davies?

"Nope, I haven't seen or heard from any of the locals yet. Communications are a big part of our problem. I suspect Captain Davies will take control here, at least until BLM decides to take over. What are the biggest needs for you guys up in Genna?"

"Water, lots of water. The Town's water supply failed." They walked over to the large map on an easel where Tristan pointed out landmarks. "There is a reservoir just north of town pumpers could fill at, but the fire is burning up that way. Partway down the hill, here, we could cut over to Salmon Run, by the covered bridge and fill up in the river, but that would likely take us out of the action for an hour to do it. If we have enough crews, that's doable. It looked as though that canyon is burning too, though I am not sure which direction. Where the hell is the air support?"

"We are working on it. Choppers refused to fly because of the winds and initially the supertankers wouldn't drop blind. I think we are beyond that now. We have them loading and scrambling now. None of us imagined this thing would move this fast, we're behind the eight-ball, but we will stop this fire."

"Better pray for rain, this beast isn't playing by our rules. Hell, it's not even playing by the laws of physics. I need a break. My guys need a break."

"Help is on the way; you guys can bunk up here and get some rest if you want."

"Not sure I am going to sleep for quite some time, Chief. When you see Captain Davies, let him know I was here." Tristan turned and walked away, stopping to grab another bottle of water on the way out.

He heard the tech, David, call out to Oliver, "Chief, we're in business. Satellite feeds are coming in now."

"Thanks, David, let's see what we're dealing with."

Tristan walked back to his guys, near the engine. They were a solid team, dutifully getting tools and hoses properly stowed while the pumper filled from a fire hydrant. He was proud of them. He wasn't sure they had made much of a difference today, but he was proud of their effort. He was about to tell them to go take a few hours and get some rest when he saw a man in uniform approaching him.

"I saw you guys protecting the evacuees along Ridgway. Thank you for stepping up and staying on the job."

"I suppose that's why they pay us the big bucks." Tristan joked. Many of the guys fighting that fire were volunteers. His crew gets paid, but definitely not in 'big bucks'.

"I was wondering if I could ask you one last favor."

He glanced over at his guys, who were all paying attention now. "Sure, what's up?"

Thursday 12:43 pm - Genna, ID

It had been two hours; the bus still hadn't come. Holly, Phyllis, and the rest of the Walgreens refugees were getting restless. Holly had voiced a contention that she could have walked down the hill by now. That may or not have been entirely true, but she didn't feel like she could have left Phyllis. God knows Phyllis could have never made it.

"Does anyone smell smoke?" one of the men from behind her said. Holly couldn't see who it was.

"No, why? Just everything that we have ever known is on fire, why would anyone possibly smell smoke?" Came a tired and frustrated response from the guy sitting across from Holly.

"Don't be an ass, this is new. Something has changed. You don't smell it?"

Holly stood up, "I need to stretch my legs anyway, I'll take a look."

"No, you can't wander back there. It's against our policy." Robert said with a mixture of fear and authority in his voice. He still sat handcuffed to the pipes of the small shopping cart corral.

Natalie, "Robert, I think you have lost whatever meager authority you used to have here. So, Shut up!" She looked at Holly, "I'll come with you. Let's look around."

The two ladies strolled toward the back of the store. Wandered through the outer aisles, checking the walls and the hanging drop ceiling for any signs of smoke or fire. They saw nothing out of the ordinary. Natalie took a quick walk through the back stockroom and the pharmacy. Though it was a bit warmer back there, she saw nothing alarming. AS she came back out onto the sales floor, Holly called out to her, "I guess I'll go to the restroom while I'm back here." She headed over to that narrow hallway and found the women's room. She locked to door, and peed, it wasn't until she went to flush that she realized that there was no water. As she pulled he pants up, she instinctively reached over to the brick wall behind the toilet for balance. It took her a moment to notice, but the bricks were hot... very hot. She pulled her hand away and got herself zipped up to get out.

She exited and called out, "Officer Horne? I think I found something."

She turned toward the men's room and put her hand on the door.

Natalie turned the corner, into the corridor, at that moment. She saw Holly just as she got to the door and yelled, "Stop! Don't ope...'

Holly had pushed the door open, releasing a burst of fresh oxygen to the starving fire. The pent-up energy released as a massive flare right into Holly's face. Her instincts made her fall back into the hallway as the fire chased her out. She felt an impact as something landed on her. She soon realized that it was Natalie, throwing herself over Holly to protect her from the fire.

The flame retreated after the initial flare-up, back to its consummation of the men's room.

"Are you okay?" Natalie asked.

"I should be asking you the same thing. Thank you." She noticed tiny black spots along the Officer's neat, blond ponytail. Singed but not burnt, thankfully. "OMG, we are on fire now, where are the busses."

"I don't know. Let's grab some waters from the case and take them up to the folks up at the front, then I'll try to get a status update."

They grabbed a couple of cases of water and hauled them up front. As Holly broke them out and started handing them out, Natalie went out the front door with Officer Mathews. Holly could see them talking into their microphones, but they looked frustrated. When Holly ran out of water bottles, two of the guys ran back to grab another couple of cases. Holly decided to get some answers. She walked out the front door.

"I'm going around back to see how much the building is burning." She said without slowing down. She turned the corner. Officer Matthews tried to stop her.

"Ma'am we can't let you do that."

"I don't believe that I asked for permission. Nor do I have to. I need to know where we stand."

Matthews trailed her around the building, while Natalie was still talking into her mic, but pacing far enough to see them around the corner. Flames still surrounded the building, their tiny oasis.

"Ma'am, stop. It isn't safe out here."

"I'll tell you what isn't safe, sitting in a solitary building for two hours while our world burns around us. Now the damn 'safe space' is on fire. What would you have me do? You promised us a bus, but it isn't coming is it? I could have walked off this damn hill by now, but you wanted to keep us 'safe'... Nobody on this mountain is safe." She rounded the back corner, the building was brick, but the wooden eaves over the drive-thru had caught fire and spread to the roof. Even the shatterproof glass drive-up window was melting out of its frame. The mortar between the bricks was smoking terribly. This was bad. Really bad.

"Come back around to the front and let me fill you in, ok. It may not be safe, you're right, but it is infinitely safer than being back here right now, at this moment."

Holly relented with a sigh and a heavy weight on her shoulders. They were probably going to die here. She turned and walked with Officer Matthews.

"We aren't getting a bus, are we?"

"We've been promised one. It was supposed to be here thirty minutes ago."

"Can't you get a status update?"

"Don't tell anyone inside, but about an hour ago, our radios went silent. No communication."

"But I just saw Officer Horne talking to someone, was she just bullshitting us?"

Natalie chimed in to answer as they got to the front of the building. "No, I'm not trying to B.S. anyone. We can't hear anything, but there is a chance that they hear us. I just reported our new... situation.

And the fact that we're all alone here." She looked around.

Holly hadn't even noticed when she had been so eager to get around to the back, the streets were empty. No sun. No traffic. No firefighters. Just some downed power-lines and a handful of burnt or burning cars. The Ridgway traffic jam had cleared. They really were stuck here.

Natalie broke the silence, calm and in control, as always. "We're going to go back in there and try to keep folks calm. We'll keep an eye on the fire and when the time comes we will decide whether it is safer in there or out here. Right now, it is safer in there. But pray. Pray the bus gets here soon."

They filed back into the store. Holly, once again, sat and comforted Phyllis. Natalie and Matthews updated Officer Rivera. As they did this, Natalie had an idea.

She walked over to the cart corral, "Robert, how many fire extinguishers are in this place?"

"I don't know." He thought a moment, "maybe four or five that I can think of. Why?"

"Four of Five? This building is what eighty thousand square feet? There has to be more than that." She dismissed him and wandered, still thinking.

"More like sixty-eight thousand. There's one by

183

the front register. One in the back room. One on a column on that middle row. One by the bathrooms and one in the hallway by the offices. We used to have more, but when we put the sprinkler system in we took some of them down."

Natalie steeled herself and with a confidence that she didn't feel, spoke to the crowd. "Okay folks, the bus is on its way. That's the good news. The bad news is that the fire has reached the back of the building and broken through into one of the bathrooms. This is a big building and mostly brick, so I think we have enough extinguishers to slow its progress until the bus gets here. The most important thing is for all of you, except for three volunteers to stay together and stay right here. If things go badly, we won't be able to search the store for you. If that happens, when I give the signal, we'll all go out the front doors, together and in an orderly fashion. Got it." She got a few tired nods from the crowd. That was enough. She grabbed a bottle of water and took a swig. "So, I need three volunteers, who is willing to help?"

"What do we have to do?" came a voice from the back of the crowd, a twenty-something kid who had had his earphones in the entire time they had been there.

"Help us keep that fire at the back of the store until the bus gets here."

"Nah, man, I ain't no firefighter."

"Then sit down and shut up."

Holly stood up. "I'll do it."

Two other men looked at each other then stood. "I'll do it." They said in unison.

Natalie had her team, the three of them and the three volunteers. They had a plan. It was something. Something to keep her mind on and focus on. "Okay, let's gather all of the fire extinguishers into the center aisle there." She pointed toward the center column, and the six scattered to collect them. Natalie grabbed the one off the column next to the cash register, dropped it at the center aisle, then went towards the office. She didn't see one in the hallway and decided to search inside it. The darkness made it tougher in the windowless room, she pulled her small Maglite and swept around the room. She opened the solitary small closet door and found shelves overflowing with old marketing materials and assorted store supplies. She was about to close it when she noticed, on the floor under the bottom shelf, a red cylinder. She bent down to get a better view and saw that there were five of them, dust-covered, but worth a shot nonetheless.

She stuck her head out into the hallway and called out," Hey guys, I found something. Come give me a hand." She started pulling the extinguishers out and lugging them into the hallway. The guys came and grabbed them, and they gathered at the center of the store. They had ten extinguishers, for the six of them. Granted that some of the dusty old ones from the closet might not work, but they would soon find out, and soon.

"Matthews and I will take the bathrooms and hallway in the back. You guys spread out along the back wall. Save your shot until you see flames. We are out of options after this. Thank you, guys, for stepping up. Let's do this."

They all nodded and separated, taking up positions along the back wall. Holly headed straight for the pharmacy, where she had seen the window melt away. The four foot by eight-foot window was gone now, she couldn't tell whether it had really all melted out, or if it had given in to the extreme temperatures and simply shattered, but either way, it was gone. Beyond it, the fire was in full consumption mode as it ate the overhang of the drive-thru. Its tentacles reaching this way then that, licking every surface that it could reach. She stared at the beast. It seemed to stop and stare back.

The wooden window trim was burning, but it hadn't breached the interior, yet. The window sat only a foot above a Formica-covered wooden counter and less than a foot to the right was the first row of medications. She frantically began sweeping everything off the counter-top: paperwork, notepads, prescription sheets, even the two computers, anything that might give the fire purchase inside the building. She cleared the shelf too. It was heavy steel shelving, so she figured that clearing the medicine boxes and bottles would make it less likely to catch. A single sweep, of her arm across each shelf, brought it all crashing to the floor. It wasn't elegant, but it was highly efficient.

When she turned back toward the window, she realized her first mistake. Just inside the left edge of the window opening was a bulletin board covered with safety information and employee communications. One flaming tentacle had apparently reached into the room, now most of the paperwork was burning. The flames spread quickly from the board to the shelves that ran along that wall. It was time to fight. She pointed the pin and squeezed the handle of her extinguisher, aiming first at the quickly spreading shelf, then back towards the bulletin board. The white powder doused the flames quickly. She kept squeezing as she aimed at the burning window frame, but the wind blew most of it back towards her. She changed angles and tried again. Still, most of it blew back into the room. Not wanting to waste her limited resource, Holly released the trigger and stepped back a bit to wait for the next incursion.

Officers Horne and Matthews gathered in the hallway, outside the men's room door. "You kick it open and aim high, I will aim low. We'll see if we can stop the flare-up. But be safe."

Matthews nodded in return. They pulled the pins and got into position.

"Three, two, one...Now!"

The door slammed open, as they pulled their triggers simultaneously. Matthews went high and took much of the flare from fresh oxygen into his face, but it was a momentary lick from the fiery beast. He fought the ceiling fire, which covered ninety percent of the room Natalie slid in on her knees spraying low and in a wide arc from the wall on the left to the center of the space. She was screaming a warrior's yell, in her head, she honestly couldn't tell if she was screaming out loud. Her senses were overwhelmed by the wind, smoke, heat, and the sound of the fire combined with the extinguishers' whooshing noise. The marble floor was scorching hot, but as she got further into the room, she could see the walls hadn't caught fire from inside the bathroom, the fire was inside the walls and breaking out into the bathroom.

Realization hit, "Shit, get out!" She grabbed Matthews by the back of his shirt and pulled him back out the door. Between them and the main sales floor stood the door to the women's restroom. It hadn't been burning before, she hadn't even thought to check when they had come back to deal with the men's room. The ladies' room shared a wall with the men's. If it had escaped while they were in the men's room, they might have been trapped. It stood before them intact. They hurried down the hall to get clear. As they passed, she placed her hand on the door; it was so hot that she instinctively pulled her hand back from it.

"What do you think? Do we hold here and wait for it to break out? Or should we go attack it, like we did the other one?"

Matthews hesitated a moment, "Honestly, while I think we made a dent in the other one, I bet it is already burning just as fiercely as it was. Let's prep and hit it once it gets through that door. I'll go grab us each another extinguisher. We'll need them handy when these peter out."

"Okay, I'll stand ready."

She stepped out and shouted to the rest of the gang. "How's it going out here?"

"Nothing going on over here." Replied the guy along the cosmetics wall.

"I have some smoke, but nothing to fight, yet." Said Officer Rivera.

"I am going to need another tank and some help soon," cried Holly. "The pharmacy is wide open now, it's only a matter of time."

Natalie looked at guy covering the far-right wall,

by the freezers and coolers. "You see anything?"

"Not yet."

"Grab another extinguisher and go help in the pharmacy." She watched him hustle back to the middle of the store to retrieve a tank.

Matthews had arrived with fresh tanks, just as the fire in the bathroom burst out into the hallway. Not through the door, but through the wall next to it. It punched through and immediately began to grow along the wall fueled by fresh oxygen and new materials to burn. Natalie opened up, aiming for the hole in the wall. She extinguished the initial flame almost immediately, but the flames had now broken through in several more spots. She sprayed for about ten more seconds until the nozzle began to emit white foamy retardant, signaling that it was now finished.

Matthews stepped in and took her place, while she retreated to grab a new one. She came back up beside him and pulled the trigger to add her stream to his and fight the flames back. She pulled the trigger. Nothing happened. She quickly looked at the gauge, which showed it in the 'green' range, but nothing was coming out. "Damn." She muttered she smacked it the tank with the heel of her hand and squeezed the handle again. This time it came to life throwing a white cloud of retardant into the hallway. Five seconds later, it started to fizzle again. She smacked it again and the gauge fell to zero. She tossed it away. The tank Matthews had was running empty at the same time. He grabbed the second one and began to spray, but this one too was old and had no pressure.

Natalie shouted for the cosmetics guy, "Bring that one over here."

He hustled over and began to pour his extinguisher's contents down the hallway. Rivera heard the call and brought his over too. Natalie went back to the center aisle and grabbed the last two extinguishers from the floor. She turned to Matthews, "This is our last gasp, you go back to the hallway, I'll go see how they're doing in the pharmacy."

She could see as she approached that the battle for the pharmacy wasn't going much better than the battle of the bathrooms. Both Holly and the other guy, Dillon, she thought she had overheard at one point, were standing firm and giving their all. Unfortunately, the fire had encroached the ceiling here now, too. Natalie rushed in and launched the last tank of retardant at the flames. The three of them standing side by side spraying the beast before them brought a bizarre flashback to watching Ghostbusters as a kid, she briefly wondered what dimension might open up if they crossed streams. She wasn't sure it could be worse than the dimension that she was stuck in at present.

Holly's tank was the first to run out, as the spray became a dribble, then... nothing. Dillion's extinguisher languished similarly moments later. Natalie kept spraying and shouted for the other two to head back up front where it was safer. Holly hesitated briefly, not wanting to leave her alone here, but followed Dillion back to the front of the store.

Natalie fought until the last burp of retardant slid from the extinguishers hose, determined to do everything in her power to save these people, and herself. When it was done, she dropped the empty tank to the floor. Her head dropped to her chest, in defeat. She was sweating profusely, she was filthy, and she was angry. Where was the damn bus? How are we supposed to help these people without a miracle? Then for the first time, she had the thought, I don't want to die here. She hadn't even considered her own survival at all today; she was just doing her job.

Desperate to change this line of thinking, she stepped back out of the pharmacy. She untucked her uniform's shirt and ripped it off before releasing the Velcro which held her bulletproof vest on. She wasn't particularly worried about someone shooting her today. She let it drop to the floor and began walking toward the front. Her sweat-drenched t-shirt finally getting some air, cooled her down a bit. She stopped by a cooler on the way and grabbed a few bottles of water, opened one and took a long swig. She still had a job to do, and she would do it.

The rest of the officers and volunteers had gathered back up front again by the time she got there. She let out a deep breath. She looked at Rivera, "Call in our status, please and remind them we need a damn bus. I don't know if they can hear us, but we have to try."

"Okay everyone, obviously the back of the building is burning now. We slowed it down, but it is inevitable. We will stay gathered here until either the bus gets here, or flames and smoke become more dangerous in here than they are out there. If you believe... hell, even if you don't, now would be a good time to say some prayers. Have faith. Does everyone have some water?"

She leapt up and sat on the checkout counter and did her best to look relaxed and patient. She felt none of that on the inside. From her vantage point, she watched as the flames spread out onto the sales floor, in an unstoppable march toward them. As it spread, the noise grew as it got to products that popped, sizzled and exploded from the heat. She looked at Robert, the pathetic assistant manager, he was meek and full of fear. She jumped down and uncuffed him. "Run if you want, but you will be safer if you stick with us."

Watching the flames grow evermore entrenched and engulfing the back half of the store now, she had the thought again. I don't want to die here. Her patrol car was parked right outside, but she could never live with herself if she abandoned all these people. I'm sorry Daddy.

She waved Matthews and Rivera over and whispered, "Why don't you guys take your car and get out of here? I will stay with them. Go home to your families. Well, maybe not home, but go be with your families."

The guys glanced at each other, made eye contact and knew the answer was unanimous. Matthews spoke up, "We're in this together. We're not going anywhere." Then he smiled, it was out of place, but perfectly timed, "Besides, I'd rather die here than face your Dad after leaving you here. Not going to happen. Besides, it isn't over yet. We still have a chance."

Natalie smiled and laughed, "Wuss."

She heard a faint siren though the fire's roar, cocking an ear she could tell it was getting closer. She jumped to her feet and headed out the front door. She could see lights coming in their direction. A firetruck burst out of the smoke and flame with a trail of water spraying from the back-end. She saw a firefighter atop the speeding truck manning a hose, spraying it directly behind them. A moment later a bus broke through the inferno, it was the target of the spray. The bus, whose header read Department of

Corrections had it's own watery escort, to keep it safe. The engine pulled in and stopped well beyond the Walgreens, allowing the bus to pull up in front of the store's entrance. The bus was scorched along the sides, but she had never seen such a glorious sight. Until the bus's door folded inward and the driver stepped out.

It was Sheriff Horne.

Natalie squealed, "Daddy!" They embraced as only a father and daughter can. "We didn't think anyone was coming. We tried to stop the fire, but couldn't."

The firefighters hustled into the store to assist in getting the stranded evacuees up and moving.

"I know, baby girl. I came as soon as I could. The unions wouldn't let any of their bus drivers come up here, into the fire. So, as Sheriff, I hijacked one of my own. Then I had to find an escort, those guys are genuine heroes." He looked her in the eye, "So are you. The composure that we heard over the radio, even knowing that you weren't getting a response... I don't know what to say. Except, I am so proud of you."

Tristan led a line of people out the doorway, towards the bus. They looked tired and still scared, but the sense of relief that crossed all of their faces when they saw the bus and the beloved Sheriff was plainly visible. Except for Robert, he didn't seem at all relieved to see the Sheriff. Holly stepped out of line and gave Natalie a hug, and smiled at the Sheriff.

"You've got quite a daughter there, Sheriff."

"No, Daddy, Holly here stepped up when few others would have and fought as hard as anyone. She's a hero." Ezra shook hands with Holly.

They followed the last ones onto the bus. Matthews and Rivera, along with a couple of firefighters, did a final sweep of the building to make sure nobody got left behind.

With everyone on-board, her father behind the wheel, and their watery escort leading the way, Natalie stood at the front of the bus. "I know it's a tight squeeze folks, but make the best of it. Thank you for your patience. What do ya say we get out of here?"

A roar of cheers and applause met her words. Smiles found a number of faces that had not been exuberant all day.

Chapter Seven

1:47pm - Rome, ID

After they dropped Walter, with a surprisingly uneventful departure at his lady friend's place, James and Josh decided to find a place to hole up and regroup. They needed to figure out not only, what the hell had just happened, but what was next. What do you do, when everything is gone and completely out of your control? They had helped as many people as they could, now what?

They found a coffee shop around the corner. Both headed straight back to the bathroom to attempt to wipe some of the sweat, soot, and grime from the morning off their faces. The place was crowded, an odd mix of lookie-loos, survivors and journalists camped out for the big story. James found it interesting that none of the journalists seemed to be speaking with the survivors, but were absorbed in their own standard Starbucks experience of coffee and WiFi.

James grabbed an empty table out on the patio, while Josh stopped to shake hands and console a few constituents. People were already looking for answers, but James knew that Josh didn't have any. All they really knew was the few places and things that they had experienced. He knew that, as much as he had seen and experienced the last few hours, it was only a fraction of stories that would eventually be told about this day. He feared a large number of the stories would never be told. Josh took the seat across from him. Strange as it seemed, despite the smoke and the sirens and the traffic in the parking lot, the patio was much quieter and peaceful than it had been inside.

"So, Mister Councilman, did you have all the answers for your adoring fans?"

Josh laughed, "I know nothing. Honestly, I was at that intersection directing traffic pretty much since the fire breached the canyon, that's all I know about. Though I assume that if it was that bad there, well, I'm not sure I want to know the rest. Where were you, before I saw you?"

"I got around a bit but saw more than I wanted to. I was actually heading to your office, to see you, when I saw the smoke. I thought I would check it out and tried to get over to the canyon by the hospital. Never made it past Starke, I ended up helping direct traffic there for a while. Then when that area cleared out, as the fire took over, I saw this amazing young girl running through the fire. I picked her up and we went to get a few of her friends that had been left behind at the school when it was evacuated. We then got trapped by the flames and ended up driving through the cemetery to get to Ridgway. My car didn't survive that, a fire crew put it out and took the kids off the hill. I kind of wandered downhill, until I saw you. The whole friggin' thing is too surreal to comprehend."

"Yeah, I keep hoping to wake up from this nightmare. I don't think that I am going to."

"I wonder, how many didn't wake up? This thing hit awfully early in the morning, for some people. This is bad, man. Really bad."

"I need to figure out what's next. How to address this, to the people."

"Have you heard from Gillian or any of the town hall folks?"

"No, I saw Ezra Horne for a while, but not a word from anyone else. He has State Troopers helping close the roads off, and has requested National Guard units to help."

Josh looked up and saw Michael walking into the coffee shop, "Hey Mike, did you and the family get out okay?"

Michael looked and smiled at seeing a couple of familiar faces. "Hell, we were both down here already. I never even got back up the hill. Is it as bad as it looks?"

"Worse," James replied. "From what I saw, I would say the town is eighty percent gone, maybe more." Josh nodded his agreement.

Michael pulled out a chair and joined them. "I figured this place, right at the bottom of the hill, would be a good spot to find info. How long do you think they'll keep us out?"

"Until the fire is out, at least a few days, I would imagine. Until they decide that it's safe."

"I need to get my dogs. They're still in the house. You're on the Town Council, Josh. Can you get me up there?"

"Not right now, trust me, you really don't want to be up there. In a day or two, I will see what I can do." Josh watched his friend deflate at the news. "It's bad, Mike. Nobody can do anything at the moment. Hell, we don't even know anything except the areas that we witnessed. Perhaps lots of areas were spared... but I wouldn't count on it. This was a tidal wave of fire that washed over the whole town. I fear that nothing will be quick."

"So, what do we do, now?"

"I have no idea. Find a place to stay for tonight and figure out what's next tomorrow, I suppose."

"Not as easy as it sounds, I just called every hotel for a hundred miles. There's not a room available anywhere," said Michael.

"Yeah, I guess dumping thirty thousand people into a small town isn't going to be easy to handle. There's gonna be a lot of people sleeping in cars tonight."

Josh stood, "I think I need to go call my wife then find the command center, probably at the fairgrounds and get some answers and details. Once people stop cheering each other's survival, they are going to want answers. You good here, James?"

"Uh, yeah, this is fine. Not like I have anywhere else to go, anyway."

"Ok, text me first thing in the morning, if they get this thing put out tonight, I will take you two up with me in the morning to see what we are dealing with."

3:30pm - Command Center- Rome, ID

"Ladies and gentlemen, please have a seat. I know that you have a lot of questions, I will do the best that I can to answer some of them. Please understand that I don't know a great deal more than those that just evacuated, yet. But please get settled so we can start the briefing."

Ezra had showered and changed into a crisp clean dress uniform before calling the press conference to order. He sipped from a bottle of water. He thought carefully about how he would handle this. Cool and collected, that's what I need to project. Stay calm. Don't speculate, just give them the facts.

"Good afternoon, I am Sheriff Ezra Horne. It has been a difficult day for everyone here in Bear County. What has now been designated as the BonnFire began about six twenty-five this morning down off if Bonneville Road, approximately twenty miles from where we are standing right now."

A reporter from the back of the room called out, "Do you know what caused it, Sheriff?"

"Please keep questions until the end, I will answer whatever I can. But no, we don't know the cause. Today was about survival and protecting as many citizens as we could. Today is not the time to start pointing fingers." He sipped from his water bottle.

"As I was saying, the initial report of the fire on Bonneville Road came in at about six twenty-seven this morning. This fire combined with the extremely high winds and a long and dry summer season combined to make this the fastest and most intense wildfires that anyone I have spoken to had ever seen. In an hour and a half, this wind-driven fire traversed two canyons and about seventeen miles to breach the upper rim of Genna." His voice cracked and he started to tear up.

"Once it reached the top of the ridge, the fire exploded into more than two dozen spot fires along the eastern edge of town. At that point with far too few personnel to effectively fight the fire, the mission of the first responders evolved into aiding in the evacuation process and trying to protect as many of Genna's citizens as possible, as we tried to get nearly thirty thousand people off of that hill. Over the next four hours, the fire engulfed the vast majority of the town." The crowd finally fell silent. He paused for a moment to gather his thoughts.

"I want to start by thanking our first responders. Members of the BCSO, BearFire, Idaho State Troopers, and the Genna PD stood their ground and fought valiantly to ensure that as many people as possible were safely evacuated. Multiple fire crews from around the state are on their way up the hill now to fight this fire with hundreds more on their way from all over the western US. The Bureau of Land Management or BLM is bringing its assets to the area as soon as possible. Immediately following this press conference, I will be asking the Governor's office to declare a State of Emergency, which will enable us to tap into additional resources to aid us in fighting the fire and starting the recovery process."

"I was just informed that the Red Cross is in the

process of setting up a large shelter at the Neighborhood Church and more will begin getting put into place. We will get you that information as soon as we have it."

"I have called a mandatory evacuation for the entire ridge from Salmon Run Road up to Mt. Heyburn. I have requested the National Guard be deployed to help us enforce the evacuation and seal the area off."

"That is really all the information that I have at the moment. Today is hard. It is likely the first of many hard days ahead. I will update you frequently on the situation and try to get citizens any pertinent information in as timely of manner as possible. Please be patient. Help each other. We are all in this together. God bless us all."

Chapter Eight

Friday 5:00am - Rome, ID

Thousands of displaced evacuees woke up; in motels, on cots at the Red Cross shelter, on couches at friend's homes, in RVs, in their cars, even in tents hurriedly erected in the Walmart parking lot. Thousands more never slept as they relived the vivid visions of their horrific escapes. Still, others were in agony as they mourned the loss of loved ones and friends. They didn't yet know how many had perished in the fire, but because of how early in the morning the fire struck, and the lack of any functional warning systems, they feared the number would be enormous. Perhaps into the thousands. But as with most things in the chaos of the disaster, nobody had any real idea.

Tristan Byrne counted himself as one of the ones that hadn't slept. He had made sure that his crew had bunks and took some sack time. He had stayed on the fringes of the command center most of the night, watching as information and satellite imagery finally began to flow and attack plans began to be developed. There were more than five hundred crews on the Ridge battling the raging fire at the moment, with over a thousand more expected to arrive on scene this morning. Too little too late for Genna, but they still had a massive fire to fight.

There had been a real fear, in the early evening, as the fire burned towards Rome that they would have to evacuate Rome as well. Finally, they caught a break as the sun set. the still strong winds shifted a bit to the north and the fire followed, chomping a new path out into the forest. Thankfully, the population out there was minimal. Unfortunately, there was also a great deal of fuel to burn.

In the cool air of a November evening, the smoke had settled down into the valley. For most of the day, yesterday it had remained at an altitude well above Rome, giving off an amber hue to everything but not severely impacting the population's breathing and health. That change would become the new normal for the coming weeks.

It was just after five o'clock in the morning when Tristan called his crew together. He quickly updated them on the current status of things before loading up and heading back up the hill. Though the fire was technically out in Genna, Tristan's crew had been given orders to search out hot spots and ensure that there were no flareups that might either cause further damage or threaten the firefighters chasing the fire into the forest. Tristan and the guys were eager to go see what had become of their hometown. Nobody spoke much on the way up Ridgway, past the roadblocks and into Genna itself. What met them there would silence them even more.

Though the sun hadn't quite breached the horizon, it was brighter than it had been all day the day before. The smoke was more brown than black, and it had spread out across the county instead of covering the Ridge like a towering, solid black top hat. The smoke was still thick enough that they snapped their masks into place. The lack of trees was immediately noticeable. It had been a pine-covered mountain town, now the roads were littered with small, charred chunks of what had been mighty trees and telephone poles. They passed the first ruins: a completely flat lot covered in ash with a portion of a garage door laying in the driveway and half a chimney sticking up. They passed the ruins of a church with only a steel spire protruding from the ash.

There were no true 'ruins', for that word implies that something remained. This fire had burned extraordinarily hot and consumed whatever it caught. Along the left, the health clinic and credit union looked untouched, but the next six buildings had been completely leveled. Tristan almost missed the turn onto Benson, for all the landmarks were gone. As he maneuvered the pumper back into neighborhoods, the destruction got even worse. Ten, fifteen, twenty homes in a row were gone, followed by a solitary house that appeared unscathed.

"My God, it's like the old pictures of Hiroshima after we nuked it," Tristan said to nobody in particular.

They wound their way to the east; toward where they had started knocking on doors in the early battle for Genna. They passed the hospital, while most of the outbuildings were gone, the main hospital seemed to be intact. A few streets later he turned off Pulga back into what had once been a nice neighborhood, running along the lip of the canyon. The inner portion of this neighborhood was decimated much like the other neighborhoods that they had driven through, but as they turned a bend and followed the road along rim itself, several had, in fact, survived. Tristan counted two clusters, two homes in one and a little further down a cluster of three that remained untouched.

"Remember when the fire exploded on us and we had all those spot fires? It looks like once they got across the street that they joined and destroyed everything. But on the lip, if it didn't catch right away, then they had a chance. That's awesome."

"Hey, look. That's the house that you ripped the front gutter off of." Tim exclaimed, "It survived. You must have caught that at just the right moment because it never caught again."

Simply finding a few still standing, in a place where they had stood and fought to save them, had brightened the mood a bit and boosted morale.

"Let's search all the surrounding lots for hot spots and water them down as well as we can. We want no flare-ups. Let's save these five, even if we never find another standing home."

The five men got out, grabbed their crowbars and prods, and began to sweep the adjoining properties probing beneath the ash, looking for smoke and still smoldering remnants. There were still several hot spots on each lot, they marked each one and signaled to Tim when they were ready for him to hit them with the fire hose.

Tristan was drawn to a lot several doors down, the one where he had seen the elderly lady that had already passed away before he was able to get to her. Her face had haunted him during the night. He used his crowbar in a sweeping motion in the area of the master bedroom trying to find her. There were no studs or drywall left. The ground was littered with thousands of nails, which seemed weird until he realized that when all the wood and drywall burn, nothing remains but the nails that held it together for all these years. It looked nothing like the home he had been inside of yesterday morning. As he moved through what he thought was the bedroom his probe clanged on something metallic. He used the point of the probe to get under the edge and flip the two-foot square steel grate over. The disfigured remains of the lady stared hollowly at his feet. It seemed the grate and other debris had protected her head to some extent. The majority of the skin, hair, and muscles were gone. All of her body below her clavicles was gone, only her shoulders, neck, and head remained. He knelt down beside her. Through her slack, unattached lower jaw he saw her tongue was still there, though badly mottled and hued in black and a deep dark purple. Tristan walked back to the truck to grab an orange traffic cone to mark her location. He stopped near her mailbox, intact and surrounded by pristine freshly mowed grass, and took a picture of the house number with the cone in the background on his phone.

He and the boys spent the next hour probing for hot spots and flushing them with water. Tim screamed from across the street. Tristan couldn't see him from where he was but sprinted toward where the sound had come from. As he came to the backyard of the former home he saw why. Tim had inadvertently stepped onto the top of a septic tank, that had been weakened by the heat of the fire. He hadn't fallen in, but was stretched across the gap on his hands and feet; his equipment and suit made it difficult for him to maneuver his way off without falling in.

Tristan and one of the others each grabbed an arm and lifted him up backward and up onto his feet.

"Boy, you do get yourself into some shitty situations, don't ya." Tristan joked.

Tim just smiled, remembering how many times he had saved Tristan from dumb stuff the previous day. "Yeah, eventually you'll get caught up."

The guys all laughed, grateful that they didn't have to ride with him after falling in.

"Alright guys, let's get loaded up. We need to refill the water in the truck. I also want to notify the Sheriff that we need a coroner out here to recover her remains. I wonder how many more there will be."

Friday 6:15am - Genna, ID

Jillian raced up the hill. She needed an opportunity to assess the level of destruction before the Town of Genna could officially make any statements. She also needed to secure her office, if it still stood. Her assistant, Marcus Moyer should have been there fifteen minutes ago. The soldier manning the barricade had tried to keep her out, but she wasn't playing that game. By the time she was through with him he was likely going to have a new PTSD diagnosis, but not before she laid down her orders for him and made him repeat them back to her.

"Yes, ma'am. Nobody goes in or out that isn't a first responder or working for IEP or AT&T: not council members, not business owners, not reporters... nobody."

"Very good, thank you." She said as she closed the door to her Mercedes. He had hustled over to move the barricade that was directly in front of her car.

Though the median and lands along both sides of The Ridgway were scorched, for most of the drive it didn't look too bad. Then she hit the Town Limits and everything changed. It looked like Hiroshima after the A-bomb was dropped. She slowed dramatically as she dodged IEP workers, power lines and trees in the road. Despite the darkness courtesy of the smoke layer, what she could see was horrific: homes flattened, apartment buildings scorched, commercial buildings as rubble. She passed the health clinic and a credit union which appeared unscathed, but they were the exception. The majority of buildings were simply gone, a stray chimney remained from a family's home. She had prepped herself for this, or at least she thought she had. This eclipsed her wildest nightmares. She felt a teardrop but quickly quashed that emotion. *No time for that crap, I have a job to do.*

Jillian pulled up to Town Hall, which somewhat surprisingly still stood. The fresh paint and new sign had just been done within the last month after some schmuck had used the dry, peeling old sign as a symbol of the Town government's inefficiency. The large rectangular brown building appeared from the front to have been spared. She quickly pulled into her spot, Marcus' little gray Honda Accord was parked next to it.

She entered the building and made the trek to her office, heels clicking on the old wooden flooring and echoing down the hallway. The smell of smoke was strong, but not overwhelming. She would have to get someone in to clean it shortly. Her office and conference room were just before the Council Chamber, something that she had added in the first of her twelve years as Town Manager. It sent a message, in her mind, that everything that happened here was run by her office first. Symbolism was a lost art in small towns, but in this case, it was more substantive than just symbolic.

She could hear the sound of file cabinet drawers being opened and emptied. Marcus was busy. Back in her office, the smell of fresh-brewed Jamaican coffee overtook the smoky smell out in the hallways. She put her Gucci bag into the bottom drawer of her desk. There was no power, but she'd had Marcus buy a bunch of lanterns last night and these were dispersed throughout the office with thought and consideration. Marcus was nothing if not efficient. Within seconds of her butt reaching the seat of her over-stuffed office chair, Marcus arrived with her mug fresh and steaming, made with precisely one and one-quarter teaspoons of sugar and a tiny splash of heavy cream. Marcus always shined; primped, tailored and groomed to an almost unhealthy extent. Today was no exception. Despite their new state of homelessness, he could have been pulled from the pages of GQ or LGTB+ quarterly.

"Good Morning, Marcus. You seem more chipper than I would expect after all of this."

"I was pretty distraught last evening. I stayed at an old friend's house in Rome. He helped get me calmed down, then he helped me re-frame this entire mess into an amazing opportunity. I am actually excited at the prospects for the future."

"You're excited that the entire town burned down? I think you are in need of medical intervention."

"Don't be ridiculous, not because the town burned. Because of the opportunities we have to rebuild it the way we want it."

"Seriously, you need to get help. I don't have time for you to have some kind of psychotic break today."

"No, no, no. Hear me out. What has been holding us back for so long? Lack of a sewer, which is resolved. It will also be much easier to acquire those empty lots now that nobody lives there. Our other problem has been all the retirees and those families mired in multi-generational poverty. They won't be able to afford to rebuild. We can change our entire voter demographic and build a nice new town of our dreams. It won't be the old Genna but something shiny and new that will attract the middle class and upper-middle-class from Rome, Council, Spokane, Couer d'Alene, even Boise. With a disaster on this level, we are likely to get State funding and even Federal Grants to rebuild. But you, and I control the process for rebuilding. If you look at it like that, it's like Christmas morning around here."

Jillian considered this theory quietly. *He's insane. But...this did simplify complying with Gavin's demands for the forty-nine properties. And, yes, a big piece of the economic woes in the business community was simply that many residents simply had no money to spend. The meth-heads could be permanently relocated to Rome and beyond, they probably couldn't get back up here even if they wanted to. It was likely that even many of the properties that had been passed down through the generations likely were uninsured. Those people weren't likely to rebuild. The elder seniors likely didn't want the hassle of trying to rebuild in their final years. Ultimately, only the more well-off residents would be able to rebuild, and those would be nice custom homes. She had always envisioned the town as an upscale suburban community, but the lack of zoning in the early days had left a hodgepodge of cottages, trailers, and mobiles mixed amongst the custom upscale homes. But this does give us the opportunity to change codes and filter the types of homes being rebuilt. I hate it when he's right.*

"I can see some potential truth in that. But first, we need to begin the cleanup. I need to make a list of people that we need to call. AT&T is supposed to be installing a temporary cell tower this morning, so the workers can communicate. Let me know when you have a signal."

"I started putting a list together of contacts, like: State legislators, Senators, Congressman, the Idaho Office of Emergency Services, the Governor, etc., so we can get this officially declared a disaster area. We'll also need to engage with Ezra Horne and his department since they are the legal authority in charge of the evacuation and security." Marcus beamed.

"Ever efficient, I'll give you that. I'd like to also call Mayor Stone, in Rome, and request some office space and the use of their Council chambers for the next couple of weeks. We are going to need to call a special meeting of the Town Council. The residents are going to be screaming for information. Not that we really have any."

"Should I bring Joanna in to help with the planning?"

"Ha, no I will tell her exactly what to do and what to say once we are ready. For now, get all the important files boxed up and we'll haul them off the hill. Shred anything that might cause us grief later. I have most of the servers, but we will need the tech guys to be ready to install them once we get an office space."

Friday 6:32am - Genna, ID

DJ braked the truck gently and stopped in front of a downed power pole, which also was next door to one of a cluster of three homes from his list that had survived. He could see another cluster ahead, it looked to be just two from this vantage point. Everything else in this neighborhood was gone.

Bud hopped out of the bucket truck wearing thick rubber gloves, trying to look like he was working with the power lines. They had waited for several hours in the predawn gloom for an appropriate vehicle. A lone lineman from the local power company had parked his truck at the rear of a large gravel parking lot next to a diner down the road from the motel and went in to have an early breakfast. DJ and Bud had taken the man down without a sound when he returned from the restaurant. His uniform shirt fit DJ fairly well, and the truck had four hardhats with company logos in the back seat. Nobody even batted an eye when DJ fell in behind two other trucks that we coming up the hill.

Bud began to unlock and swing the bucket

around.

"Whoa, Bud what are you doing?"

"Putting the bucket out, so it looks more real... ya know like we're working."

"You idiot. The cables are all on the ground, the poles all burned. How is that supposed to look 'more real'? Lock it back down and let's get on with it. There's nobody around anyway."

DJ grabbed two orange traffic cones from a piece of rebar that had been welded to the back bumper and placed one in front, and one behind the truck like he had seen other companies do. Bud jostled the hydraulic levers until the bucket dropped back into place. Though the sun was beginning its trek across the sky, the thick smoke layer made it still quite dark here. Their headlights were the only artificial light source that they had seen, this gave them great cover for their work. They hauled several jerry-cans out of the back of the truck and trudged over behind the first house. They hurried back to the truck and from the bed pulled out a long object wrapped in several tarps. DJ was grateful that the light was as dim as it was because the lineman's arm slipped from the tarp several times and dangled toward the ground before they scrambled to stuff it back into the tarp. The pair manhandled the body up to the back door. As subtlety was no longer required, DJ used his size twelve boot and a swift kick to unlock the back door.

Once inside, they unceremoniously dropped the body onto the kitchen floor. DJ grabbed a jerry-can and doused the body with gasoline, then splashed some around the kitchen and living room.

He called out to his partner, "Bud, take the other cans and go get the other two houses. Remember what we talked about, a big puddle around the nearest shrub to the house, then a trail across the back of it. That way if anyone notices that these didn't burn the first time, they can trace it back to a hot spot that flared up and caught then took the house. Got it."

Bud rolled his eyes, "Yes, for the twenty-seventh time, I've got it."

Bud was getting tired of being talked down to. Sure, he had made a few mistakes, but he was a professional and didn't appreciate the coddling. He had run with DJ in the past and hadn't seen this animosity. If the payday for this job wasn't going to be so substantial, he'd have already pushed back hard. Instead, he ducked out of the house and went about doing his job. Yesterday's accident didn't help. He had tripped over the hose at the gas station, dousing himself before turning off the nozzle. When the fire that he started to ensure the home a few doors down burned as it merged with the wildfire, his fuel saturated pants had ignited when the first ember breached the lip of the canyon and hit his leg. It was an accident, but the job got done. He glanced over at the home in question, three doors down as if to confirm that the job had been well done. Flat as a pancake, nothing but ash and an orange rubber cone. Wait, what? He'd have to remember to ask DJ about the cone after he finished this job.

DJ had just finished dousing the first home when Bud came back from doing the other two. They loaded the now-empty jerry-cans into the back of the electric company's truck and DJ grabbed a handheld propane torch from his bag and handed his torch's twin to Bud. They walked over to the first house.

"Start down at the far one, and just light the shrub that you chose as your ignition point, then let the gas do the rest. And, Bud? Try not to set yourself on fire today, huh."

"Fuck off, DJ."

The fences had all burned down, which gave DJ a good line of sight to keep an eye on Bud. As soon as Bud's fire began to spread, DJ lit the ignition point of the second house. The dried shrub lit instantly, Dj stood watching for a moment waiting for it to make the leap to the house. Once it did, he hustled down to the first house and held the torch to the base of that shrub. Right as it ignited, Bud came up behind him.

"DJ did you put three cones out, or just two?"

DJ didn't know what he was getting at, "What

cones? The ones from the truck?" Bud nodded in the affirmative. "Two, why?"

"I wonder who put that one there. Isn't that the second one we visited yesterday, with the horses?" he said, pointing through the gloom.

DJ was torn, now that the fires were burning, they needed to get the hell out of here. But the cone in the middle of the ash pile called to him. He ran over to the cone and a chill ran down his spine. Staring up from the ashes was Marilyn Reese, number two on the list that he had been given. Mrs. Reese hadn't wanted to sign his release of mineral rights, not that he blamed her, but that had caused him to escalate his visit. Ultimately, she signed, but it was also her last act as the sedative he'd injected eased her to sleep before the poison did its job. Now she was haunting him with her skeletal ghostly presence. She was so frail that he was certain that her body, and any evidence of his actions, would have burned completely in the heat of this fire. But clearly, he was mistaken.

"Come here, give me a hand."

Friday 7:15 am - Rome, ID

Michael and James met with Josh Florini at the same coffee shop that they had been to the day before. Mixed emotions wracked all three of them;

both eager to go see what remained and fearful that it will be as bad as they think... or worse.

It had not been an easy night. Unable to find a hotel or motel, Michael and his family had slept on couches and the floor in the home of his seventy-four-year-old Mother-in-law's new boyfriend, some forty minutes outside of Rome. Sleep hadn't come easily, nor did it last long. But he was grateful that they had a roof over their heads and a warm shower this morning. James had been able to secure a rental car yesterday and slept in it, right here in the parking lot of the coffee shop, though he looked as refreshed and energetic as he always did. Josh, luckily, had recently closed escrow on a property here in Rome that he intended to fix up and flip. It was a bit torn up, but he was able to get his wife and kids settled and as comfortable as could be expected under the circumstances. All three were well aware and grateful that they had it much better than many survivors of yesterday's tragedy.

They loaded into Josh's Lexus and set out up The Ridgway. The amber haze caused by the brown layer of smoke that now covered the entire valley gave things an eerie glow in the early morning light. Within a mile they came across the first blacked patch of grass, a former golf course that had fallen into disrepair, covered in tall grass and weeds it had been an eyesore on what was otherwise normally a beautiful drive up the mountain. That problem had been resolved; fire took care of the weeds and grass. The long straight fairway that ran along the road was a deeper, smoother black than the surrounding fringe. It looked like a rural landing strip for small aircraft.

"Holy crap, I knew it burnt down this direction last night, but I had no idea that it came this close to Rome," Michael said from the backseat.

"This may have been back-burned, to keep that from happening. I am sure they poured all their resources into keeping it on the hill. Evacuating Rome would have been even more daunting than Genna. Although there are a lot fewer trees and a lot more concrete in Rome."

As they approached the large stone gates that once was the entrance to the dying golf course, they came to the first barricade spanning the width of the road. Three National Guard troopers, decked out in full camouflage fatigues and armed with M4s stood ready. Josh pulled the SUV up to the barricade.

"I'll go talk to 'em," Josh said as he jumped out. He walked up to the guard standing at the center of the barricade.

"How are you guys doing? We need to get through."

"The town is under mandatory evacuation orders."

"I understand that. I'm Josh Florini. I'm a Town Councilman in Genna. It's official business." He reached for his wallet in his back pocket to bring out his ID. The motion caused the soldier to reach for his rifle slung across his back. Though he relaxed when the wallet came out, it clearly demonstrated to Josh how on edge these guys were. He held his ID up, but the guard had no interest.

"This area is closed down until further notice."

"I am not a civilian, I'm a Town Council-member. This is my Town and I am going to assess the situation."

"I am just following orders."

"Whose orders?"

"The Sheriff and the Town Manager."

"Wait, the Town Manager issued separate orders from the Sheriff? She works for the Council; she can't order us out."

"Again, this area is closed down until further notice. Please get back in your vehicle and move along."

Just then three large bucket trucks pulled up in the other lane, the other two guards swung the barricades aside and let them through without a glance.

"I thought this place was closed down. What gives?"

"They are with Idaho Electric Power. Lots of power lines on the ground up there."

"This is absurd. Who is your Supervisor?"

"In this setting, I have no idea. I am following orders. Good day, Sir."

Josh stomped back to his car and slammed the door shut. "They're keeping us out, too. I'm not sure why. Let's go down to the command center and talk to the Sheriff."

Friday 8:14 am – NICF Incident Command Center (Bear County) Rome

Josh stormed into the Command Center, looking for answers. He didn't like being shut out. It had been a constant on the Town Council. As the outsider, he often found himself getting emails and information at the last moment before votes and completely cut off from the process at other times. Jillian was especially wary of him, at least that is how he read her short temper when he was over talking to her staff, needling them for information. Now that he hadn't gained any new allies on the Council during the election, he expected to be shut out even more. But he resolved not to do so quietly.

He had dropped Michael off back at the coffee shop, but James had opted to come along. As they walked in, they were taken by the flurry of activity: filthy, sweat-drenched firefighters coming off shift were being debriefed. James had been so caught up in trying to see what had become of his hometown that he had forgotten that these guys were still fighting a massive wildfire. It had burned nearly forty thousand more acres overnight. The wind had subsided a bit and shifted north, but while the forest fire was burning away from population centers, it also was going through much more difficult terrain. That made it a real challenge for them to even get into a position to fight it.

Josh walked past the NICF command area and head to the back corner of the building where the Bear County Sheriff's Office had set up. Their main office was only a mile or so from here, but the Sheriff wanted to be close to where all the incoming data and information was. As they approached, Sheriff Horne was sitting on a stool in front of a free-standing olive-green backdrop littered with logos of the BCSO across it with alternating hashtags that said '#BearStrong' and '#BonnFire'. Several TV cameras were focused on him as he gave a quick morning update.

"The Red Cross shelter was overflowing last night, but more resources will be in the area today. We will get more shelters set up. No town can be prepared for thirty thousand people to descend upon it. But many people in Rome generously opened their homes for people to stay in guest rooms and on couches and floors. We are all in this together. IEP will be setting up their own base camp for their workers to stay as they assist in the cleanup of Genna, that will free up some hotel rooms for evacuees. Food will be available at the Red Cross shelter, and a number of churches for those in need. We are working on compiling a list of those now."

"The mandatory evacuation orders for the Town of Genna and surrounding areas on the Ridge will continue to be enforced in the coming days. I took a drive through Genna this morning. There is a great deal of debris on the roads, many trees have fallen and downed power lines are everywhere. IEP and their contractors will be assisting in the cleanup at this stage, as we try to make the roads passable."

Stephanie Marquez, a news reporter from Boise chimed in, "Sheriff, do you have any idea when people will be let back up to their properties?"

"I have no idea, at this point. It's a mess up there. We will see what kind of progress crews make in the coming days. I will continually assess the situation and revise or amend those orders as the situation on the ground improves."

"Sheriff, there have been reports of a second ignition point for these fires, can you speak about that?"

"The fire started down off Bonneville Road at approximately six twenty-five a.m. NICF and BLM are currently investigating the cause of that fire. There were reports of a second ignition point in the canyon under the eastern rim of Genna, but we have no confirmation, nor evidence supporting that at this time. Look, yesterday was about evacuating as many people off that mountain as quickly and safely as possible, now we will begin to look for answers. I want to commend the local first responders on the scene, and a few civilians," he glanced over at Josh and James with a nod before continuing, "for stepping up and keeping people as safe as possible during that evacuation amidst horrible conditions. That's all I have to report at this point, God Bless."

The Sheriff stood up and walked off-screen. Josh and James met him at his makeshift office space. "Hi Josh, good to see you." The two shook hands before the Sheriff turned to James. "It's James, right?"

"Yes, sir. Nice to formally meet you."

"I heard a story about a lunatic, named James, launching a flaming car full of kids off a ledge at the cemetery. Since I saw you out there directing traffic, I am guessing that you are the same James."

"Indeed, it is possible that I fractured a traffic law or two. Sorry." James smiled; Ezra laughed.

"Well done. Those kids are safe and with their families today because of you."

"Thank you, sir. I experienced more than my share of lunacy yesterday, as I am sure many did."

Josh piped in, "I was with you most of the day yesterday, and all morning this morning. Why haven't I heard any of that story?"

"Because if I tell you, it's egotistical. But if Sheriff Horne tells it, well... it is more believable."

"Anyway, I have a full plate this morning. What can I do for you?"

"I got turned away from the checkpoint. The guard said he was just following orders from you and 'the town manager'. What gives? I have constituents that want updates. How can a Town Council member be kept out of his own town?"

"My order was a blanket order covering everyone who isn't a first responder or IEP. It didn't specifically exclude you. It is almost impossible to get around up there Josh. It is even worse than you can imagine. It looks like a war zone where both sides lost. Give it a day or two and I will give you a pass that will get you through. The thing about Jillian leaving orders is a bit bothersome though. She has no jurisdiction over any of that."

"Right, technically she works for the Town Council. That doesn't give her the authority to exclude the council members from anything, even ones she doesn't like."

"We have a pretty good working relationship, but she can be a wee bit too controlling. I will clear that piece up."

"Gee, ya think? Okay, thanks, Sheriff."

As they walked toward the entrance they paused by a just updated poster-sized map that was being attached to the wall. The header read, in large bold block letters, Burn Scar. It showed a massive swath of black cut through the forest; reaching from nearly Rome, up through Genna and over across several canyons wrapping around Bear Canyon Lake. All that pristine, beautiful natural landscape scarred for decades to come. Eighty-three thousand acres burned so far and still spreading.

As they walked to the car, James had a thought. "Do you want to wait for the Sheriff to clear you? I think I have a way for us to get up there if you want to go."

"No, I have a legal right to be there. I am going to fight it, and bring light on the situation from here. If I go up there illegally, it undermines my position. Thanks though. If you go, send me some pictures."

"Will do."

<u>Chapter Nine</u>

Friday 3:34 PM - Genna, ID

Tristan and Sheriff Horne drove to Genna in the Sheriff's vehicle. The lack of landmarks and trees confused Tristan to some extent, but they eventually found their way up Pulga Road and back into the neighborhoods along the canyon's rim. The smoke seemed to be heavier again, and the diffused lighting had an effect on how things looked, too. After a couple of false starts and wrong turns, the Sheriff could see the tension in Tristan.

"Son, are we in the right spot? I have an entire county that I have to keep from imploding."

"I'm sorry Sheriff, but this is right, but it just doesn't look right." Then he saw it, "There it is, see that cone up ahead?" The Sheriff pulled up to the curb.

Tristan showed him the picture on his phone

with the mailbox and the cone, "See, this is it. Something still feels off though."

They got out and the Sheriff followed him around the side of the foundation of ash, to where they had to walk the shortest distance in the toxic ash to the body. They stepped carefully toward the orange cone, but Tristan could tell it had been disturbed. When they got there, his fears were confirmed… the body was gone.

"I don't understand. It was right here, Sheriff. I swear it was. What the hell is going on?"

"I wonder if an animal could have taken it?" the Sheriff began scanning the area, "But I only know one animal that would take it while wearing work boots. Did you get a picture of the body?"

"I started to, but it felt inappropriate, so I just took this one, of the mailbox." As he turned the phone towards the Sheriff, something in the picture caught his eye.

"Hey, look at this!" The Sheriff came over to look closer at Tristan's phone, "I knew something felt wrong when we got here, but I couldn't put it all together. Look, that house was still here this morning, see the blue corner of it in the pic? As a matter of fact, I think there were three in a row that were still standing. What the hell is going on?"

"Flare up maybe?"

"Sheriff, what are the odds on having the only three standing houses on this stretch have separate flare-ups and burn."

"Let's go take a closer look."

They walked over to the first of the three lots, Sheriff Horne knelt down and held his hand just above an ash-covered cinder block. He could feel the warmth. He reached down and touched it, "It isn't hot, but definitely still quite warm."

Tristan examined the ash footprint of the former home. "Yeah, this fire didn't burn anywhere nearly as hot as the BonnFire. Look, there is still some unburnt wood along some of the baseboards. There was no wood left in any of the other properties that I looked at, none at all. These were a separate fire, no question."

"There is still a question as to whether it is man-made or something else."

"Yes, but the missing body and these late-burns seem to draw a conclusion that they are, at least, very suspicious. But let's go check the other two."

They went down to the other two properties and found the same things: warmth, smoldering and incomplete burns.

"This is nuts, who would do such a thing after everything else is gone?"

"I don't know, but I am going to find out."

"Hey, up around that bend there were two more homes that survived. Let's go see if this is an isolated incident."

"Okay, I want to mark this area off as a crime scene first, then we'll get some fire investigators and a detective up here." He popped the trunk of his cruiser and pulled out a large roll of yellow crime scene tape. He tied one end to the mailbox on the elderly lady's house. He checked the mailbox, there was a mailer from a local casino addressed to Marilyn Reese. He slipped the card into his rear pocket, then unreeled the tape all the way across the front of her property and the next three.

They jumped back in the car and cruised up around the next bend, passing a lone electric company truck coming the other direction. They quickly found the spot, as smoke was still rising and a few small final flames were finishing off the job.

"Well, I'd say we can absolutely rule out random, coincidental hot-spot flare-ups. What is going on here?"

"Let's mark this one-off, then go find that electric truck that we passed and see if they have seen anyone else up here today."

Friday 3:47pm - Genna, ID

He saw the light bar too late.

"Look straight ahead and do not make eye contact." He cautioned Bud.

But as the cruiser came alongside them, DJ trying to act nonchalant turned his head slightly toward them and gave a polite nod. But even in the dim light, he could see that it wasn't just some deputy, it was the Sheriff himself.

Oh shit. Why did I look at him and nod? I just warned Bud against doing the same thing.

He kept watching as the cruiser never slowed and continued up the road.

"Okay, no problem. Just another electrician on the road."

"Deej, we might have a small problem... Look!" he pointed to the crime scene tape.

"Crap, how could they have possibly found it already? We have to get away from here, now!"

He hit the gas and raced away, swerving around debris, power line, tree limbs, and burned cars far quicker than was safe. Being prudent wasn't nearly as important as distance, in DJ's head anyway. He raced down Pulga Road, passed the hospital, and turned right onto Benson. The narrow winding road here was littered with burnt-out cars and trailers. He slowed as he saw flashing lights ahead, lighting the whole area up and flashes of reds, whites, and blues reflecting and refracting off the smoky gloom like patriotic strobe lights. DJ glanced down Edgewood as he passed, it looked like an apocalyptic movie set. On the single-lane road sat a line of what looked to be six or seven vehicles parked in formation. Unlike all the other burned cars that he had driven by, he suspected that the people in these cars hadn't had the time to escape from their vehicles before being swept up into the fire. The level of first responder activity suggested the presence of more than a few victims.

They continued past Edgewood and through a few more curves and bends before coming out on Starke Road. They turned left to head down the hill and off the Ridge.

Once they got to Rome, they knew that they needed to dump the bucket truck. They pulled into Home Depot and parked alongside an older brownish-gold Ford pickup truck with a ladder rack on it. DJ parked between the truck and the entrance to the store, effectively blocking it from view with the larger bucket truck. DJ went to work hot-wiring the Ford, while Bud sneaked between rows and pilfered a couple of different sets of magnetic car door decals; one for an electrical contractor and one for an AT&T installation contractor. These places were always a rich smorgasbord of customization items or in this case vehicular disguise modifications. Less than sixty seconds after shifting the large truck into park, they were driving away in the Ford work truck. They would switch the plates from another location and be good to go for a couple of days.

Friday 3:51pm - Genna, ID

Ezra and Tristan had run the yellow crime scene tape, then hurried back down the way they had come to find that electric truck. The truck had disappeared, which only seemed strange because they had to dodge numerous power lines on the way out of the neighborhood. They went north on Pulga then cut across to Starke Road. The sight that met them spoke to the futility of their search. Along this stretch of road, the Sheriff saw no less than forty crews from the electric company clearing downed poles and lines for as far as he could see in either direction.

He pulled alongside one of the workers standing out in the road working with a large spool that was attached to the back bumper.

"Morning, who's in charge of all of this out here." The Sheriff asked.

"Hey Sheriff, I'd say Mother Nature is in charge, but I am guessing that that's not what you mean. Umm, I guess that would be Roger. He's..." he stood up straight and turned partway around, pointing south. "He's down in the parking lot of Albertson's coordinating crews as they arrive. He'll be in or around the trailer that they hauled up here, probably. "

"Thanks, stay safe." He drove off, headed to Albertson's. They pulled up near the trailer and walked up. They could hear a raspy and rather bellicose voice carrying over the noise of diesel generators and the back-up beeping of trucks maneuvering into position.

"No, stop and listen to me. I want you to take these three poles and the areas between them on that side of the road." He turned to another man, "You and your guys take these five, here. Got it?" They were all looking at a blown-up map of the electrical grid which was taped to the side of the steel trailer. A large whiteboard was also fastened to the wall, upon which he scribbled their truck numbers into their assigned spots. "Get to it! We have a shit-ton of work to do. Come see me when you finish." The men nodded and left for their assigned posts.

Ezra cleared his throat, "You must be Roger."

Roger was a short, but solidly built man who looked to be in his mid-fifties. His blue button-up company shirt was already smudged with smears of soot and ash. Ezra could immediately see that he was a worker who had moved up to this position, as opposed to one of the corporate-type managers that one often sees.

"Sheriff." His response both an acknowledgment and a question.

"There was an incident up on the northeast side this afternoon. There was a bucket truck of yours doing some work nearby, but he was gone before we got back to try to talk to him and see if he had seen anyone or anything in the area. I'd like to talk to him."

Roger moved over closer to the map. "Where were you when you saw it?"

Ezra examined the map and pointed, "It was a two-man team and we were right about here."

"When did you see them?"

"Not more than ten minutes ago."

"That doesn't make any sense, did the truck have a logo?"

"Yep, it was one of yours."

"Weird. I don't have anyone working even close to there."

"Are you sure?"

"Of course, our mandate for the next week or so is simply to clear the main roads: Ridgway, Starke, Benson et cetera. We have nobody even on Pulga yet, certainly not back into any of the residential neighborhoods. It wasn't one of mine. My guys are all accounted for."

"You don't think that one of them might have run back to see their property or something?"

"Look, Sheriff. My guys know that I am an overbearing asshole who watches everyone and everything. They wouldn't risk it. They might run into this neighborhood, right here, for thirty seconds, but no way any of them would wander off that far away from their assigned posts. I can't explain what you saw, but it wasn't one of my guys."

"Don't you guys have a bunch of contracted workers coming up here?"

"Yes, but they are all headed inbound today, they are to report to the IEP base camp at Tuscan Ridge golf course where we will plan for larger operations tomorrow. These guys up here today are all local crews."

"Okay, thanks for your help."

The Sheriff and Tristan walked back to the car, deep in thought. He really wished the transmitter was up and working. Then he realized that they had been able to hear his daughter yesterday, even if they couldn't communicate with her. He picked up his mic.

"Dispatch, this is Sheriff Horne. Issue a county-wide APB. Dozens of Idaho Electric Power bucket trucks are on the way up to the Burn Scar area. I am not interested in those. I am looking for an IEP bucket truck with two male occupants heading out of the area. Stop them and send me a picture, then await my response. Word it however you need to, just get it out now. I am on my way back to the Command Center."

"As if this catastrophe isn't bad enough, now we have a potential murder, five arsons, and a missing body. Can't wait to see what tomorrow brings." Tristan shook his head. "I just can't believe it."

"It's likely to get worse before it gets better."

Friday 4:15pm - Genna, ID

DJ and Bud drove slowly, waiting for a couple of IEP trucks to exit the golf course base camp onto Ridgway, before falling into line behind them on their way up the hill. With their 'electrician' door magnets in place, they followed the caravan through the checkpoint without a 2nd glance from the guards. There were now so many IEP contractors, that the security was not capable of being anywhere near as tight as appearances might suggest. DJ had long made a career of acting like he belonged, wherever he was. Sneaking around attracted attention, but acting like you belonged made you invisible in all but the strictest security environments.

They had had to bail early this morning due to that damned Sheriff's patrol car. He still had no idea how they discovered the crime so quickly, but either way, they still had work to do. They had laid low and prepped the truck with fresh plates and more fuel for much of the afternoon, just to make sure the heat was off. But DJ knew that law enforcement had much more important things to deal with in the aftermath of the fire than actively looking for them.

Just after they turned onto Benson, his phone dinged, indicating a text message. The screen simply said, 'Call Me'. DJ looked at his signal strength and was surprised to see five bars or full signal. They hadn't wasted any time getting that sorted out. He pressed the 'Call' button.

There were no formalities, "What is your status?"

"We are just getting back into town, we had to leave early this morning due to an inconveniently timed Sheriff's patrol. We have changed vehicles and restocked our supplies to finish the job."

"I drove through a little while ago, there are still six of your list of forty-nine that need to be dealt with."

"Wait, you're here? How did you get in?"

"Never mind that. I am concerned that they may identify a pattern if all the homes that burn are

242

located along that ridge. So, choose three more standing homes randomly throughout Genna and torch them as well. Understood?"

"Boss, I understand. That does make this much more dangerous for us. It's one thing to sneak around on the outskirts, but to burn some within the town creates much more exposure."

"Do it. If they are still standing tomorrow morning, you won't be standing anymore. Do I make myself clear?" came the crisply enunciated voice in response.

DJ sighed. He had no choice. "Yes, sir. But that will cost you more."

"Get it done." The phone disconnected.

<u>Chapter Ten</u>

Saturday 6:30 am - Rome, ID

Michael came back to the base of the hill. Day three of staring up the hill, completely helpless. On the forty-minute drive in from where they were staying, it became clear that the smoke had thoroughly settled from the upper atmosphere, down to ground level. The news on the radio discussed, not the fire itself, but the air quality. From Boise to Portland, apparently, people were wearing face makes to try to filter out the toxic smoke. While he understood the fears for people with asthma or emphysema, he didn't understand why people far away took this very personal tragedy and made it all about them. He had seen many people in Rome wearing masks yesterday and this morning, but the smoke hadn't bothered him enough to even worry about it. He had even seen one guy wearing a mask, but he had cut a hole into it which had his cigarette sticking out of it. Talk about absurd contradictions.

Yes, it was smoky. There's a big fire on the hill, what did people expect. He didn't know quite how to deal with this co-opting of impact, but he was a writer, he coped with it the only way he knew how; he pulled out his laptop and walked over to sit at one of the coffee shop's outdoor tables and began to put it into words.

Ten minutes later he sat back and reread what he just wrote, it was by far the best work he had ever produced. It had flowed from his heart to his fingertips and bled onto the screen.

An UnFiltered Breath

In the aftermath of the Idaho wildfire that destroyed the town of Genna, talk around the state has turned away from the tragedy and onward to air quality warnings for the entire State and much of the Pacific Northwest. And perhaps rightly so. There are indeed dangers to breathing the smoke-filled air. Masks are recommended anywhere within 100 miles of Genna.

But sitting here... a mere 9 miles down the hill, below my beloved home, my perspective is a bit different. Though I am smart enough to realize the danger, I breathe unmasked. For me, it isn't simply toxic smoke. For me, that smoke carries much more...

That smoke, that so many complain about, carries the last remnants of my Beloved Town. That smoke, that so many complain about, carries the last remnants of friends and neighbors. That smoke, that so many complain about, carries the hopes and dreams of every small business owner on the Ridge. It carries churches of every flavor. It carries away the faith of some, while strengthening the faith of others. It carries our parks and beautiful vistas, scarred for now, but not destroyed. It carries the invincible innocence of every child that should never see the sights they saw that day.

If you listen closely, that smoke is made up of every song I have ever written & recorded and every word I have ever written. Its chemical composition includes my favorite artworks of my children: handprints, paintings, their first written words... Everything.

That smoke carries within it the last remnants of my pets; Macie, Connor, and Sammie. It carries my high school letter jacket and football helmet, my favorite guitar, that painting on the wall, and my photos of life. Lost baby teeth, clippings of hair, all the things of no value that mean everything. It carries my home.

That smoke carries the same pains that my friends and neighbors are suffering, it is a truly shared experience. That smoke carries the Thanksgivings of 30,000 and the memory of what it was to be.

That smoke carries what is left. When the smoke dissipates there will be nothing left. Except, what is in our hearts. Love of Genna. Love of each other. Love of the potential of a rebirth.

So, yes, I am an idiot for not conforming to the masked masses' sense of preservation. But I will continue to find my own perspective, my own peace, my own memories. I will breathe my unfiltered perspective.

Yes, that captured his feelings perfectly.

Saturday 7:15am - Genna, ID

Sheriff Ezra Horne stood over the still-smoldering remnants of yet another fire. Captain Davies and Tristan Byrne stood next to him, a crowd of first responders was growing behind them. This was the fourth location they had visited already this morning.

"Kori, is there any chance that these are natural flare-ups?"

"It's possible. But I wouldn't count on it. The thing is that hot spots can flare up days after the original fire, but it would take a perfect set of conditions for it to flare in a burned footprint and leap to an adjacent unburnt structure. It can happen. It does happen, but not like this. Not with, what, ten or more structures... that we know of. No way, the odds against this being natural are astronomical. You have a firebug on your hands. These are deliberate."

Ezra knew this to be true, he was just hoping that there might be another explanation. He had a great deal on his plate. He, in his role as the County Coroner, was meeting with the first of his search teams later today. They would begin the property-by-property search for victims. Due to the early hour of the fire on Thursday morning, many suspected that there might be thousands who perished. He hoped that was outlandish, but with the population scattered across the Northwest seeking shelter, it was very difficult to pinpoint how many were missing at this point. Either way, that part of his job, he really wasn't looking forward to. He definitely didn't need an arsonist added to the mix.

Yesterday evening, a Rome police officer had located an abandoned IEP bucket truck down at the Rome Home Depot, while investigating a report of a stolen vehicle, a brown Ford Painter's truck. The floor mats in the bucket truck had smeared ash footprints on them. The driver assigned to that vehicle had not reported to work yesterday. The evidence was mounting.

But if they dumped the bucket truck yesterday, how did they get back into Genna overnight to torch these houses?

He waved two of his deputies over, he looked at Deputy Juarez first. "I want you to map all of these suspected late burners. Then coordinate with him," he pointed to Deputy Thompson. "Who is going to find five or six other deputies that are standing around with nothing to do, and divide the town up. I want you to drive every neighborhood that you can access and look for any more partial burns, like this one. They stand out from the BonnFire structures because the heat isn't nearly as extreme so there is usually something left: a piece of wall, a stairwell, something that looks different from the flattened ash piles that the wildfire left behind. Got it."

"Yes, Sir."

"I want you two to coordinate and map any additional late burns and see if we can come up with any trends. Report back to me by one p.m. We need to get out in front of this." The two nodded and headed out.

Captain Davies stepped up close to the Sheriff. "Before we split up, we have something else we need to discuss, privately." The Sheriff looked around and walked back towards the canyon rim at the back of the property, with Davies and Tristan in tow.

"What have you got?"

"Inspectors found something at the origin point, that you need to see. It is too early to tell if it is related to the fire, but we are looking at everything, especially in light of this arson business." He pulled out his phone and swiped to the appropriate picture. "It would be better if you could see it in person, but I know that you are busy." He handed the phone to Ezra.

It was a picture of an electrical transformer or at least some sort of electrical box attached to a pole with a tape measure run along the side of it for scale. He was a Sheriff, not an electrician so he didn't know the function of the metal box, but he was quite sure that the five bullet holes in the casing weren't supposed to be there.

"Hmmm, did you get any bullet fragments out of it?"

"We haven't opened the box yet. We're waiting on IEP to ensure it is discharged and dead before we touch it. But we did dig this out of the wooden pole just below the box." He pulled a baggie out of his breast pocket and handed it to the Sheriff. It was bullet; misshapen, but intact.

"My guys think it's either a .22 or a .223, it is tough to tell. But you're the expert with this stuff."

"I'd guess .22, but we will let the forensics guys run the ballistics. Did you find anything else?"

"Still waiting on paperwork from IEP, but from what we have, it appears that the hook that fastens the transmission line to that tower hasn't been replaced in nearly a hundred years. It looks to be original to when they first ran power to the area. Maintenance has never been a huge priority for them, it seems. Without the bullet holes, I would say that the likely cause of the BonnFire. With the bullet holes, well... it's too early to make that call. Certainly, that transmission line falling into the dry grass is what started the fire, at least for that origination point. We just don't know, for certain, what caused it to fall, yet."

"Any word from IEP about why they didn't shut the power off like they warned everyone that they would?"

"Our investigation is the origin of the fire, political and corporate decisions that may have led to it aren't really part of that. That's more your domain, or the Idaho Utilities Commission's. But no, I haven't heard any reasons for the decision."

"Okay, thanks for the heads up. Let me know if you come up with anything else. I will see you guys this afternoon at the briefing."

Tristan piped in, "Okay, see you then. I have to run down to Emmett and look at a house to rent, but I will be back by twelve or one."

"Man, that's quite a commute."

"Right now, there is nothing for rent within a hundred miles and all of them that have doubled their rent since Thursday. But I'll make it work. My ride just pulled up."

"Where's your car?" the Captain asked.

"Well, ya see I was on the pumper truck on Thursday morning, it seems that my car and our station didn't make it. Maybe you remember that?" He laughed.

"Right, sorry."

A white pickup truck with door logos of a property maintenance company pulled up next to the Sheriff's cruiser. James climbed out and walked over to the group.

"James Augustine, how in the hell are you up here? Yesterday, I praised you for your heroic actions and today, you're going to make me arrest you for breaking the evacuation?"

"Easy now, Sheriff. I'm just doing my part to support the first responders."

"James and I ran into each other last night; he's going to run me down to Emmett."

"That still doesn't explain how you got through the roadblocks."

"Simple, I just acted as if I belonged and followed a few IEP trucks through. Nobody batted an eye."

The Sheriff pondered this for a moment. "That's it!"

He grabbed his phone and called the just departed Deputy Thompson, "Joe, spread the word amongst the guys to be on the lookout for any non-IEP pickup trucks. Stop them and check IDs, and IEP contracts to ensure that they belong. We might be looking for a Brown Ford half-ton with a painter's logo on the side. But anyone who doesn't have proper ID and a contract needs to be detained. Go ahead and arrest them for violating the evacuation orders, then we'll try to connect the dots on evidence for arson charges as the investigation moves along."

He called the Command Center and gave them

identical orders.

This might be our first break.

Saturday 7:58am - Genna, ID

As he headed back down the hill, back to the Command Center, Sheriff Horne noticed a couple of cars in the Genna Town Hall parking lot. He decided to pull in and update Jillian Dupree on what was going on in this town. Mercedes' tend to stick out in a mountain town such as Genna. She would be here.

He strode through the side door and walked down the hall to Jillian's office. He could hear a machine whining a few seconds at a time. He turned to walk into her reception area and Marcus, standing over a rolling portable shredder with a stack of documents in one hand and attempting to capture the machine's output in a large black garbage bag with the other, nearly leapt through the ceiling at the Sheriff's sudden appearance. Paper shreddings flew before floating to the ground.

"Jesus, you startled me."

Ezra laughed, "I've been compared to a lot of people, even Chuck Norris, but I must admit that Jesus is a new one. Where's Jillian?

Marcus had that blood-drained look of fear flash across his face momentarily, before regaining his composure. He jerked his head toward her office door. "She's in there, Sheriff."

"Thanks." Ezra eyed him as he walked by trying to determine if the fear was a result of being startled, getting caught shredding government documents or something else. Though Marcus had always seemed wound a bit too tight, so it was hard to say which it was.

"Morning Jillian." He said as he entered the office. Stacks of file boxes, stacked four or five high, had, in essence, created a partition in the middle of her office between her desk and the large conference table that adorned the far side.

"Hey Sheriff, how are you?"

"Well, we've all had better days. Do you have a few minutes to let me update you on where we are?"

"Absolutely. We're just packing stuff up to move into our Rome office space since we don't know when we'll be able to get utility services back to the building. So, pardon the mess."

She pulled out a chair at the conference table and waved to offer one to the Sheriff. "Okay, where are we?"

"We're in a helluva mess, that's where we are. I want to be open and honest with you, but some of this cannot be disclosed to anyone, yet. Understood?"

"Of course."

Marcus plunged in, "Would you like some coffee, Sheriff?"

The Sheriff declined, and Marcus leaned against the door frame to listen.

"As for the cause of the fire, most signs point to a one-hundred-year-old hook on an IEP transmission line. However, there are a couple of other bizarre circumstances that have prevented the investigators from making the call, officially."

"What?"

"First, there were a number of bullet holes in an electrical box of some sort on the same pole that the transmission line had been attached to. We don't yet, know when that happened or what impact, if any, the bullets had on starting the fire. Second, there have been reports since day one about a second origination point for the fire up closer to the Ridge. We haven't found any evidence of this, and given the strength of the wind that morning, if there was one it was likely an ember from the primary fire. Or so we thought."

"What do you mean, 'or so we thought'?"

"Since the fire, so, in the last thirty-six hours, at least ten houses that survived the BonnFire have been burnt to the ground. We don't know why, but we're on their trail. Some of my guys are driving neighborhoods looking for additional late-burns to add to the list. We have some leads, and I saw one of them, briefly. We didn't know we were looking for anybody when I saw him. We'll find them."

"Who would burn homes in a town that already lost everything?"

"Speaking of losing everything, I am meeting with the Search and Recover team later today. We will begin searching for victims tomorrow. We have already found five victims still in their cars over on Edgewood, and one over off Pulga Road. She, a Marilyn Reese, was found during the door to door search but was already deceased before the fire. It seems that her body is missing. I think it is connected to the arson fires."

"Why do you think they are connected?"

"She lived right next door to the first one that we discovered."

She glanced over at Marcus, wide-eyed, "That's horrible. Are you sure the fire didn't get her?"

"One of our first responders found her yesterday morning. By the time he got me out there mid-afternoon, it was gone. Which leads us, of course to the question of: Why?"

"Why, what?"

"If she died of natural causes or from the fire, why would they need to dispose of the body? The only reason would be if they had something to do with her death, in the first place. And that leads us to another, why. We'll find them. They aren't nearly as slick as they think they are."

He stood up and feigned straightening his already perfect uniform top. "Well, that's about all that I have. See ya around." He began walking away, then turned back suddenly, catching Marcus flush white again. *This kid needs to toughen up.*

"One more question, Jillian. When did you become a member of law enforcement?"

"What do you mean?"

"I mean, that I am the only person in this county with the legal authority to order an evacuation, and deploy staff to enforce said evacuation. Don't you ever try to bully one of my guys again. You do not have the authority to issue orders to anyone, except Marcus, here. I don't play politics; I do my job. Period. Your little political games in the midst of this disaster will not be tolerated."

"Wait a min…"

"No, you wait a minute. This might be your town, but it is my county. Everyone and I mean everyone is going to have to learn to play nice if we are going to get through this. That is all."

He turned on his heel and left.

Saturday 8:07 am -- I-95 South

Traffic was light going downhill on Pulga Road as one would expect from an empty town, and this route avoided any city traffic by joining I-95 south of Rome. There were many fire crews heading up the hill to continue the firefight, but they were solo on the outbound lanes.

"So, if you move to Emmett, are you going to transfer down there, or work in the Treasure Valley?" James probed.

"I have no idea. I just feel like I need a place to live. Everything else is too much to think about now. I have been running on adrenaline for three days, somewhat intentionally, so I don't have to think too much about what we've just been through. Right now, it feels like some surreal, yet amazing experience. I suspect that when I stop, the horror of it all will come crashing in. I am not ready for that yet."

Four large dump-trucks turned onto their lane, about a quarter-mile ahead of them. James glanced at his rear-view mirror, there was nobody behind him. *I just don't understand big lumbering trucks pulling out in front of someone doing seventy-five miles an hour. There's nobody behind me, it would have been all clear if they had waited for ten seconds.*

"Yeah, I haven't spent much time thinking about it. Lots of time praying, very little thinking. That's the only way that I can deal right now too. What are these guys doing?"

James pulled into the other lane to pass the trucks, but they moved over at the same time. He slammed on his brakes and shifted back to the right lane. He passed as the dump-trucks slowed even more and turned left onto a dirt road that James had never noticed before.

"Where the hell are these guys going?" he glanced into the rear-view mirror again and six more identical trucks had joined the original four. "Do you know what is up that road?"

"Not really, I thought it was just an old fire road, but it looks like it was recently widened and graded. Maybe a new subdivision or something?"

"I thought all of that was BLM land."

"It is, but it not abnormal for them to sell off or lease out a chunk here and there."

James' gut was screaming for him to go check it out. *No, I am taking Tristan down to Emmett. It is probably just nerves and paranoia, coupled with the fact that I haven't slept in over forty-eight hours.*

He shook off that thought and kept driving. A couple of minutes later three flatbed semi-trucks loaded with heavy construction equipment passed them going the other direction. James braked until he was going slow enough to make a U-turn. "Let's take a little detour. It will only take a minute. Then we'll get back on the road."

"Good, I was going to suggest the same thing. Who does construction, ostensibly in the fire zone, on a weekend two days after a major wildfire swept through? It could be innocent, but..."

As they suspected the flatbeds were headed to the same road. "Could they be clearing debris from the fire?"

"If they were working ahead of the fire, then yeah. But I assure you that with an active fire still burning, nobody is thinking about cleanup yet."

They slowed to a crawl and followed, well behind, the flatbeds. They turned onto the dirt road flanked closely by trees. A few hundred yards in they came to a fork in the road; to the left was newly graded and well used, the path to the right had random weeds and growth peeking up through the soil. James took the old path. They didn't know where they were going, but he wanted to see it before anybody knew that they were watching. He pulled in a hundred yards or so, then pulled off the track into the trees where he stopped.

"Let's hike up and see what's going on." James got out of the truck, adjusting his holster to a more comfortable position as he did so.

They could hear diesel engines, a lot of them, and a few back-up beepers. Whatever this was, it was an active site. They trekked through the trees between the two dirt roads. There were a few burnt spots, but this appeared to be the western edge of the burn scar. As they hiked deeper more and more blackened stumps appeared amidst the thinner forest. The thinner forest also meant that their cover was diminishing.

"Why don't you keep going this way? I will flank around to the right and see what we can see. We've got to be close."

"OK, just stay out of sight," Tristan warned.

James scrambled over the rock-strewn landscape, scampering from tree to tree parallel to the road above them. After about four hundred yards he turned north. The well-thinned forest and blackened trees emitted a haunting energy. His adrenalin levels had his heart pounding. Nearly fifty yards up the embankment, his view opened up and he dropped behind a boulder. Peeking his head back over the top, James could see a massive clearing and bulldozers were working efficiently to expand it further; uprooting trees and shrubs as they did so. Men scurried around the site; guiding trucks and heavy equipment to the appropriate spots. Far to the left, he could see a security checkpoint manned by men carrying what looked to James like military-issue M4s. At the far edge to the right, he noted two more security guys. It seemed like a lot of firepower for a construction site, and it was clear by both their physiques and their focus that these were not rent-a-cops.

Along the cliff-face, he could see four large vertical scaffolding towers that had been mounted in the rock. Along one side of each tower was a long track that stretched nearly the entire height of the towers, it looked to him to be well over one hundred feet tall. At the bottom was a large black box that looked like an electric motor with a Plexiglas cylinder extending from the front of it.

A man, mid-fifties, with dark black coiffed hair and dressed in khaki slacks and a button-down dress shirt directed the workers to back away. He picked up a large handheld remote-control unit, attached by a thick black cable to the bottom of one of the motor units. He pressed a button and the box buzzed to life. The whole unit rotated ninety degrees so that the Plexiglas tube pointed straight up, then launched up its track dragging a net bag below it. It stopped near the upper rim and rotated until the Plexiglas was pointing at the cliff face. The unit inched forward until the cylinder pressed against the rock, then the motor fired up as a small auger lurched out from within the cylinder and began drilling into the rock. A secondary motor engaged as the debris from the drilling was sucked through the Plexiglas tube unto a plastic tube. After a moment the drilling stopped, the unit rotated ninety degrees upward again which caused it to eject the filled and sealed plastic tube, which landed in the net dangling below the machine's body.

The machine quickly dropped five feet and repeated the same procedure, ejecting yet another plastic cartridge into the bag. Then it dropped five more and continued the process.

James was mesmerized by the process, watching this machine do precision work in this most chaotic and imprecise bit of land. *What are they doing? Gathering samples, it seems, but for what?*

At that moment he heard a sound that he would recognize anywhere, the sliding clack of a charging handle being released and sliding forward the bolt carrier group of a rifle with a freshly chambered bullet. He was about to turn around and look when he felt the muzzle press against the base of his neck.

'Now would be a good time to put your hands on your head." A gruff voice said, in a tone more polite than James expected.

James complied without a word and stood with his hands behind his head. The guard motioned forward and to the right with the gun's muzzle.

Another guard appeared and joined the procession as they marched into the site. He scanned the area and noticed it was even larger than he could see from his position behind the boulder. The guards at the entry checkpoint glanced his way, then quickly resumed their outward-facing duties. He didn't see any sign of Tristan, which gave him hope.

James still had his weapon, which was good. But he knew he wasn't a professional, he carried for defense. Even if he was, he was badly outnumbered, still, it made him feel better having it on his hip. It helped him relax in this stressful and unfamiliar situation. They led him toward a pop-up tent away from the work area. The khaki-clad man was waiting.

He looked at the guard. "Why bring him here? Your job is to keep people out."

"He was sneaking around watching what was going on."

"So, shoo him away. We aren't doing anything subversive. We just don't want people looking around." He turned to James, "So what are you doing, here?"

"I was just going for a hike and heard some activity. What are you doing here?"

"It's just an infrastructure project. But we are trying to keep it quiet, can I count on your silence?"

"What kind of infrastructure project begins two days after a town is completely wiped out? What construction project has an armed, para-military security force that likes to harass hikers?"

The man's jaw tightened, "It matters not. All that should concern you is that we are permitted and under contract with the Town of Genna."

James dropped his hands off his heads and down to his sides. He knew he was pressing his luck, but this didn't feel right... at all. "Last time I checked, this is outside of the Genna Town Limits. This is Bear County out here."

A buzzing, whirring sound broke the tension as a different man activated the drill on the second tower and began the same process.

"Actually, this is private property, on which you were caught trespassing. So, despite your obvious curiosity and a misplaced sense of righteousness, it is you that needs to consider your situation."

"Cool, call the Sheriff and turn me in. Let's see how legit your little charade really is."

From behind, the muzzle reappeared at the base of his skull. "Hands on your head. Now."

When he complied, a hand grabbed his interlocked fingers keeping them in place as another hand patted his right hip, then lifted his shirt and extracted his handgun from its holster. "What do we have here?" The man searched more thoroughly and removed James' wallet, which he handed to his boss.

The Khaki man stepped closer, "Just out hiking, huh?" He glanced inside his wallet, "Mr. Augustine." He took the weapon from the guard, ejected the magazine and cleared the chamber with smooth practiced precision.

"Yeah, it was with me when the fire hit. Everything that I own, I am wearing. Hiking is great for burning off the tension of losing your whole town. Ya know, unless you run into a band of armed lunatics drilling high-tech core samples in the burn scar. That doesn't help the tension at all."

"Son, you just don't know when to quit, do you?"

James ignored him and continued his speculation, "It makes you wonder a few things. What are you drilling for that's so secretive? What is valuable enough that you need all this security? Oh, and why were you staged and ready the moment the fire passed this area to begin doing whatever it is that you are doing? Not to mention the biggest question."

"Oh yeah, what is that?"

"Did you have something to do with starting the fire, in the first place?"

James watched closely, as he said the last one. It was a total shot in the dark, but only when he asked the last question did he see the man's jaw muscles contract and his eyes widen momentarily. It wasn't an admission of guilt, but it was an indication that something was going on, and this guy really didn't want people nosing into his business. When his eyes narrowed, James knew he had gone too far and put himself in a precarious position. James hoped that Tristan could see what was happening from his position and would go for help.

"Take him and secure him somewhere out of the way for now."

"Great! We can add false imprisonment to the list of charges."

"We are detaining an armed trespasser. It is less messy than shooting trespassers, although that would be within my rights here in the great state of Idaho. I suggest you cooperate." He turned back to the reports he had been reviewing before their intrusion.

James allowed the guard to guide him over to the far side of the clearing where his hands were fastened with thick black zip-ties. He was then asked to sit in the scoop of a parked bulldozer, his hands were then pulled above and behind his head and fastened to a chain loop that was welded to the top rim of the scoop. Clearly, it was not intended to be a comfortable position. He leaned back along the curve of the scoop in an effort to get as comfortable as possible, then closed his eyes and said a little prayer. He didn't pray for his own safety, though he hoped that would work out too. No, he prayed that Tristan had avoided detection and had been able to see enough to get him to go find help.

Fear clenched in his chest a moment later when he saw several of the security team sprinting towards the entrance. He renewed his prayer as he prayed for Tristan's safety. James had dragged him into this, it would take divine intervention to get him out.

Chapter Eleven

Saturday 8:33am - Genna, ID

DJ rolled off the couch, his legs caught briefly as the blanket had wrapped around them. Bud was snoring away in the master bedroom of the mid-sized manufactured home that they had appropriated. They had had a very long night, dodging a surprisingly large contingent of law enforcement personnel keeping watch over the abandoned town.

They had decided that leaving Genna so early in the morning would be suspicious, so they found one of the few standing homes in Lower Genna, well-away from the night's pyromaniacal activities.

The home was a fairly nice, three bedroom-two bath layout. But the key for them was the large workshop on the property that allowed them to hid the work truck. It had gotten markedly colder overnight than it had the previous three, as November in the mountains tends to. They had considered utilizing the fireplace, but caution dictated that they opt for another solution. Of course, with the power out there were no other options but to gather all of the blankets that they could find and layer up.

DJ knew he could have slept in any one of the bedrooms, but he had always felt weird sleeping in someone else's bed, at least without them being snuggled in beside him. Bud had no such qualms and sounded like a chainsaw as he sucked the wallpaper off the wall from the big comfortable looking king size bed. DJ hoped he would sleep all day, he needed a break. Bud was wearing on him and they had decided to stay here at the house, until dusk when the IEP workers would make a mass exodus down the hill. They would simply join the procession and get off of this tormented hill. Their work was done, now they just had to be patient.

It had been a long, night. DJ and Bud had torched nine homes in just over six hours. They had scoped out this house earlier in the evening so that they could make a quick and decisive entry when the last fire took hold.

DJ was starving. They hadn't planned to spend the night in Genna so they hadn't come prepared. They had found some crackers and peanut butter in the cupboard when they arrived here. The food in the freezer was still fairly cold, but without utilities, there was no way to cook anything. There was no water coming from the tap either. There were going to have to figure something out soon.

DJ walked through the living room, bored and restless already, looking at family photos on the walls. *Nice looking family.* Four children, three girls, and a boy. All dressed up for family picture day. It reminded him of the one attempt at a family picture when he was growing up. It had been planned for weeks, and DJ's mother had bought them all-new outfits, tan shorts, and teal shirts, so they all matched. His father had gone out with the boys that night and raised more than a few adult beverages. When he got home, he saw all the new outfits laid out so they would be ready first thing in the morning. He went into the bedroom and dragged DJ's mother out of bed by her hair. He dragged her all the way out into the living room where DJ slept on the sofa. His father slammed his mother's face into the new clothes which were laid out on the hardwood kitchen table. The sound of her nose breaking woke DJ from his teenage slumber, just in time to see her slump unconscious onto the ground. The blood-splattered clothes no longer pristine, his mother unconscious and the angry drunken father elicited none of the smiles that he saw in these pictures. *This must be what a real family looks like.* DJ thought before he smashed the picture onto the floor. He had never had one, never wanted one, and certainly never needed one.

He decided to go out to the shop and see if there were any bottles of water stashed out there. Bud was going to have cotton mouth when he woke, he drank two bottles of wine that he had found in the refrigerator. He was unbearable in the best of times. Hungover, thirsty and hungry was going to make for a very long day if DJ didn't have a solution of some sort.

He pulled on his shoes and slipped out the back door. The shop was a cavernous cinder-block building with a metal roof and a single rolling overhead garage door that was extra tall to allow for RV clearance. It also had a regular doorway, on the wall to the right of the rolling door, which didn't close completely due to the broken door frame from when DJ had kicked it in to gain access several hours ago. A light tap swung the door open, he left it that way to let some small amount of light enter the pitch-black garage. There was no RV inside, only an older Ford pickup truck with a ladder rack. The one that they had used to impersonate an IEP contractor and gain access to the Ridge. He reached in through the open driver's door window and pulled the headlight knob, illuminating much of the shop.

DJ rummaged through the cabinets and shelves looking for items they could utilize, but primarily for water and food. He grabbed a flashlight from one drawer and a half a pack of beef jerky from another. Despite there being a ton of stuff in the cabinets, there was little that was useful to them at the moment. Until he reached the end. Around the side of the last cabinet, in front of the open door to a restroom, he found three cases of bottled water stacked atop each other. *Eureka!*

He threw two of them into the bed of the pickup and decided to take the last into the house. He stuck the flashlight in his back pocket and balanced the beef jerky packet atop the water. As he walked out the door towards the house, he heard an engine. He quickly ducked back inside the door, the rapid change of direction causing the foil jerky packet to slide off the case of water. He watched from the inner darkness as a Sheriff's deputy cruised slowly down the street, his spotlight shining through the smoke-dimmed morning light. DJ wasn't sure if the deputy had seen him or not before he had jumped back into the doorway. He unconsciously held his breath, a bead of sweat forming on his brow as the car, far too slowly, continued down the road.

Saturday 8:45am - I-95 Corridor

He had suspected that this plan could go south, but he never imagined something like this. This kind of thing was the sort that happened in movies, not in real life. He had never imagined armed mercenaries, nor had he foreseen one of them being taken hostage. Tristan had figured that the worst case would have been to be shooed away by the guards. Clearly, he had not understood the gravity of the situation. Hell, he didn't have any idea what was going on, at all.

He had seen James marched toward the tent

canopy at gunpoint and witnessed a long conversation with the guy in Khakis before he was relieved of his belongings and zip-tied and led off, out of Tristan's sight. But not before he snapped off a few pictures on his cell phone's camera.

Once James had been captured, Tristan had settled into better cover lying prone amidst fire debris and behind a rather wide tree stump. He had even taken some soot and smeared it on his face the way he had seen soldiers do, in the movies at least. He counted the guards that he could see, there were seven, all armed with what appeared to be M-4 rifles and handguns holstered on their hips. He knew there were more. Against such odds, what could he do? He really didn't want to leave James in such a vulnerable position, but unarmed and alone Tristan couldn't think of a plan to free him. Not one that would work, at any rate.

He decided to crawl backward out of his hiding spot and head back to their borrowed pickup truck. As he did so a piece of debris dislodged and smacked against the stump in front of him. He froze instantly. Listening and watching for any change in activity on the sight.

"There's another one!" shouted one of the guards.

Several guards, already at a heightened state of alert from the discovery of one intruder, launched into an all-out sprint. The guards split wordlessly as if they had trained for this very scenario dozens of times, some coming toward his position rapidly picking their way through the debris field, while others ran straight down the path as if to cut him off from the entrance. It was unlikely that they knew his present position precisely, but it was just as unlikely that he would remain undiscovered once they reach his general vicinity. He feared that if he bolted and ran, they would be on him in seconds, but he knew that if he didn't the game would be over anyway.

"Time to face your fears, big boy." He muttered under his breath.

With his palms flat against the soil he gathered himself and took a deep breath, which he held for a beat, the exploded his hands into the ground propelling his body onto his feet and instantly began running. He wasted no time with finding cover or anything else, concentrating on putting one foot in front of the other as rapidly as possible. He knew he had to reach the truck before the guards could get there.

"There he is. Everyone converge to the southwest." Came a voice shouting into his radio.

A shot rang out and echoed on the hillside. Tristan didn't bother looking back, that would slow him down. He put his head down and ran even harder, suddenly grateful for all the endurance training that he had been put through as a firefighter. As he reached the area that was less burned and had retained much of its foliage, he began to weave back and forth through the trees. Another shot rang out, hitting a branch just to his left. He cut right.

A booming voice cried, "Cease fire! We want him alive. Go, go, go."

He could hear boots pounding the soil in his wake. It sounded like a lot of them, but Tristan dared not glance back. The truck was only another fifty yards or so. He kept pumping his legs. He was now near enough to the point that the two paths merged that he could hear the other set of guards running towards the entrance.

At last, he saw the tailgate protruding from a copse of trees. He never slowed down as he cut around them and slide to a stop at the driver's door. He climbed in and reached frantically for the ignition as he pulled the door closed. The key wasn't there. He panicked, unsure exactly how much time he had, but he knew his window wasn't shrinking, it was collapsing with every second. He pulled down the visor. It wasn't there. He checked the center console, cup holder and was about to look in the CD storage compartment when he saw it. On the floor, halfway hidden under the edge of the floor mat. He grabbed the key and cranked the engine over and immediately shifted into reverse. The tires spun as he quickly backed up and left, nearly careening into the first guard to reach him. The man leaped out of the way, which stalled his momentum giving Tristan the split second that he needed to shift into drive and punch it, accelerated away with a spray of dirt and gravel kicking up at the other guards just as they arrived on the scene.

Tristan sped down the path, eager to get back to the highway and some level of safety. He came to the junction where the two paths converged and hit the main road faster than he should have as the truck's tires lost traction momentarily. When they reconnected, Tristan was staring into the grill of an oncoming dump truck. He cranked the wheel and stomped the gas pedal, sliding around it with inches to spare. Before he even regained his breath, just twenty yards up ahead, he saw what he feared. A line of security guards, rifles lined up and ready to fire, spanned the width of the road. Instinctively, he started to brake before making the only viable choice... he floored it.

The guards scattered and he fishtailed through the turn and bounced onto the highway narrowly missing an oncoming car that he was in no position to see. He took the finger that he received with grace, he was simply grateful to be alive.

Saturday 9:02am - Rome, ID

The Command Center was bustling with activity. The NIFC still had a massive wildfire burning with only ten percent containment. Members of the press found ways to be in the way whenever possible. Commissary staff were hustling to keep the food and water tables stocked

The Sheriff had just finished his morning briefing when word came in about a possible location for their firebugs. A deputy had seen movement, however brief, at what should have been an empty home in Lower Genna. He had been smart enough not to engage and to continue on his patrol before reporting in. None of the checkpoints had seen the missing Ford pickup truck coming down the hill overnight, so they expected that the culprits had holed up somewhere on the Ridge. This might just be the break that they had been waiting for.

Ezra was looking at a map of the home in question which had been blown up and spread across the top of a folding table. He had the Chiefs of both the Genna PD and Rome PD with him as they worked to allocate resources.

"If they make a run for it, their only option will be out through the back yard, around the pond, and into the vineyard. If they make it to the vineyard, we will have a helluva time catching them." said the GPD Chief.

"We can utilize the National Guard to fill in the gaps if we need to, but we have to remember that they aren't police, they are soldiers. We'll need to reel back their instincts a bit if we use them. We can bring a S.W.A.T. team in from here and here, perhaps." Ezra pointed to two spots on the map.

A disturbance distracted the men, as a soot-covered man ran full-speed into the Command Center. Dodging other firefighters and leaping over cable snakes, Tristan fought his way through the crowd back toward the Sheriff's makeshift office area.

Thoroughly out of breath, Tristan skidded to a stop at the table. "Sheriff, I need help. They've taken him. They're holding him hostage." He wheezed before bending over and putting his hands on his knees in an effort to catch his breath. He never took his eyes off the Sheriff, though.

"I thought you were headed to Emmett. Take a deep breath and explain to me what in tarnation you are talking about. We have a lot going on this morning. We've got a line on our firebug."

Ezra had come to respect Tristan over the last few days. He was brave and willing to lay it all on the line to get his job done. It wasn't in his nature to be as frantic as he now appeared.

Tristan stood upright and put his hands on his head to open up his lungs. "Great, but James Augustine has been taken hostage. We need to go get him."

"Hostage? By whom?"

The two police chiefs were paying rapt attention now. Tristan continued, "We were heading down I-95 when we saw a whole brigade of dump trucks turning off onto an old fire road that runs along beneath the rim of the Eastern Ridge." His breathing began to return to a more normal pace. "It didn't seem right to either of us that there would be a major construction or demolition project two days after such a major fire. So we flipped a U-turn and trailed them in. We stashed the pickup and hiked up to the site where they were working; clearing the area and drilling into the cliff face with some type of high-tech drill."

He paused and pulled out his phone, opening up the pictures that he had taken. Handing the phone to the Sheriff, he continued. "There were a bunch of heavily armed security guys. One of them found James. They've zip-tied him and are holding him somewhere on the site. Then they shot at me as I tried to get back to the truck. I don't know what they are doing, but everything about the place feels wrong."

Ezra looked closer at the pictures, "Those look like M-4s, that's some serious firepower for a bunch of rent-a-cops. These guys look ex-military. What are these?" he asked, pointing to the scaffolding attached to the cliff.

"Those are the tracks for the fancy automated drills that they were using. They zip up and down and drill holes into the rock, collecting samples in a vacuum canister of some sort and spitting them out." Tristan went up next to the Sheriff and pointed at a photo on the smartphone screen. "This guy in the Khakis seems to be the leader."

Ezra swiped his fingers apart on the screen, enlarging the image. It was only a profile of the man, and grainy at this resolution, but still there was something familiar about the man that the Sheriff just couldn't quite grasp at the moment. He looked up at the police chiefs.

"Change of plans. You guys round up the National Guard boys and use them to close down the area and a single S.W.A.T. team to hit the front of the property in Genna. Do not let these guys slip out of there. I will take the other S.W.A.T. team and go knock on the door of this construction site. Aside from getting James released, I would really like to know what they are doing down there." He looked at the men gathered around him, meeting the eyes of each of them. "Any questions?"

There were none. They moved out. Ezra pulled his phone out and called his Tactical Specialist, the leader of the Sheriff's S.W.A.T team and asked him to bring his guys in for a briefing in ten minutes. Their office was nearby, they would be here and be ready.

Ezra walked over to the tech guys and had him print out large format copies of a road map, a topographical map, and a satellite photo of the area that Tristan had described. The first two took only moments before the over-sized printer began making noise. The third, however, required some discussion.

"Sir, the satellite hasn't made its pass over the area, yet today. We have pictures from around seven o'clock last night if that works for you. Otherwise, you are looking at an hour and a half or so, before the next flyover."

"We don't have that kind of time. Give me the

two you have, then send the sat feed to my phone once it comes through."

He grabbed the two large posters, hustled back to 'his' area, and again spread them out on the folding table. "Show me exactly where you were."

Saturday 10:27am - Genna, ID

"Bud, get up, man!" DJ pleaded with his still inebriated partner. In fairness, he had only been asleep for four and a half hours, hardly enough time for anyone to clear the alcohol from their bloodstream.

DJ immediately corrected himself. *But I would never drink on the job, and that's what this was. The work was done, but we are on the job until we get away. Damn it!*

His paranoia had grown exponentially since seeing the patrol car this morning. Every sound had him peeking out the blinds, certain that this was the end. However, the deputy cruiser had never come back by the house. There was an abundance of vehicle noise due to all the 'real' IEP workers cleaning up power lines. DJ had had enough, he wanted to get the hell out of Dodge, but his slumbering drunken partner wasn't cooperating. Their original plan, of just staying put until evening, had been a solid one. But the minutes crawled by like days and the paranoia had taken hold. He had checked to confirm he had a round chambered and a full magazine in his Hi-Point forty-five caliber handgun, at least twenty times. It wasn't much of a gun but it was cheap and with dozens of rubber bands stretched around the grip to limit fingerprint transfer, it worked great as a 'drop gun'.

Honestly, he never expected to need it once the fire hit. He had only brought it along for the first day of trying to attain mineral rights in a more persuasive way. If he thought he would end up in a fire-fight he would have brought his trusty Beretta PX-4 Storm.

He slammed the magazine back into the pistol's grip and checked the front blinds again. Nothing. Out of frustration, he screamed, "Goddammit, Bud. Get up so we can get out of here."

DJ was losing it. He was always the cool one, but he flinched at every snap of the American flag blowing in the wind on the pole by the front drive. He jumped at every lighting change, and with this much smoke in the air, the lighting and hue changed frequently. A shadow shifted behind the blinds. DJ closed his eyes and tried to will away the urge to check the front of the house again. Anxiety was exhausting. Paranoia took that exhaustion to another level entirely.

Bud raced from the Master bedroom carrying his boots in his hands as he tried to put an arm through his flannel shirt. "Somebody's outside my window. We need to go."

If it wasn't for the instant of panic, DJ's response might have been, *"No shit, I have been trying to wake you for an hour and a half."*

As it was, they simply both bolted for the back door. When they reached the back patio, they heard the front door being smashed in. They ran, full out, through the back yard with a bit of gratitude that the fire had burned the back fence leaving them one less obstacle between the house and the ability to disappear into the vineyard.

Once they left the grassy yard and hit the more natural wildlands, DJ began to pull away from the bare-footed Bud, who cursed with every step as if shrapnel cut through the soles of his feet. DJ was only twenty yards from the entrance to the vineyard, legs pumping as fast as he could lift them. He looked back right as he arrived at the entrance to check on Bud. He was almost keeping up. Fear was a good motivator. DJ ran through the arched gateway. Right into a well-timed and devastating straight-arm that caught him in the throat and sent his feet up in the air as he landed on the back of his head.

A swarm of soldiers emerged from seemingly nowhere with weapons locked and loaded as Bud screeched to a stop. Frustrated, he tossed his boots to the ground and raised his hands above his head. He could see DJ still clutching his throat and gasping for air until three soldiers secured his arms and flipped him on to his belly. One disarmed him, while the other two slipped a pair of handcuffs on him. Bud looked physically ill as he put his hands together in front of him to await his cuff.

Half a dozen members of the Rome S.W.A.T. team arrived on the scene and took control of the prisoners.

Saturday 12:07pm - I-95 Corridor

James slumped down in the scoop. He was tired and his back was killing him. He also had dried blood on his face that itched like crazy, but with his hands fastened above his head, there was little that he could do about it. They had moved him to a chair for further interrogation after they had failed to capture Tristan. It wasn't a pleasant time, physically. But once he realized that they were trying to find out who had escaped his psychological state improved immensely. They didn't torture him or anything. No, they just tried to rough him up and intimidate him into hand over information. When he laughed in response to their question about where Tristan lived, they realized that they weren't getting anything more out of him. He snorted when he made up an address in Genna and said, "go ahead and stop on by, I'm sure he'll be home." Knowing full well that the likelihood of any of Genna's residents having a home at this point was not even slim, but a sliver of a chance.

Instead, he told them that 'Derek' was his bi-sexual hiking partner and an occasional flower delivery person. To men like these, that description would ease tensions and the perceived threat from such a person. They seemed to like that narrative. Little did they know that James knew exactly where Tristan would go and had a pretty good idea what the response would look like.

He had really hoped that they would leave him handcuffed to the tent canopy and sitting in the surprisingly comfortable folding chair. Of course, anything was comfortable when compared to the dirt clod encrusted, curved steel blade of a bulldozer. But it had also given him a better view of the crew working on and along the cliff face. He still hadn't figured out exactly what they were up to and wanted to continue to observe. The dozer that he was now re-attached to was positioned to face away from the worksite. On the upside, while he couldn't see what they were up to, neither could they see what he was up to. He began testing the zip-ties: first by pulling both hands down together attempting to break the tie that held him to the dozer, then he worked each individual tie around his wrists. These weren't Dollar Store zip-ties. His wrists were bleeding and he had zero evidence that any of them had weakened at all.

He surrendered and tried to let all of it go. He had faith that help was on the way. He just needed to be calm and patient. He closed his eyes and took a long deep breath. He held the breath for two beats and began a long slow exhalation. He let his mind clear itself of negative thoughts as he slipped into a meditative state. He focused only on his breathing... until he felt a hand grab his. He opened his eyes as a quick snipping sound let his hands fall from atop the scoop. Tristan stood over him with a finger to his lips. He grabbed James by the ties still bound his hands and helped him to his feet.

"Come on, quickly," Tristan whispered.

As the pair made their way deep into cover, a sniper whispered into his throat mic, "Freebird has flown. Freebird has flown." Then he swiveled his scope towards the security checkpoint at the entrance to the site.

That was Ezra's cue to turn onto the fire road and pull up all the way to the barricade. He eased to a stop and got out as two security guards approached uncertainly.

"Good afternoon, gentlemen," Ezra said as passively as someone with his bearing and presence could. "Could you point me in the direction of whoever is in charge here?" He didn't wait for an answer as he walked around the barricade and into the site.

"Sir, this is private property. I'm going to have to ask you to stop here while I let Mr. Martinez know that you are here."

"Son, do you see this badge? It says Bear County Sheriff. I happen to know for a fact that this isn't private property." He pointed to his right, "all of that land belongs to the Bureau of Land Management.

The cliff face belongs to the people of Genna who own the property above it. But this road, the old fire road we are standing on, I can assure you belongs to Bear County."

More security personnel drifted toward the entrance, trying to not act in a threatening manner, but it was no random leisurely walk either.

"Be that as it may. I must ask you to remain here while I contact Mr. Martinez."

The Sheriff knew that these guys were trained to follow orders, but he also knew that there was no way that they had trained and prepared for the arrival of the top law enforcement officer in the county. That uncertainty gave him the advantage.

"You tell Mr. Martinez that he can find me over by the fancy drill riggings that you guys have." He didn't look back and continued walking towards the cliff. The additional security folks also had uncertainty written all over their faces. They encircled him but didn't try to stop him. He pushed on through.

As he reached the main work area, he saw a man wearing Khakis and a well-pressed plaid cotton twill coming toward him from the tent canopy. The Sheriff kept walking toward the cliff and the automatic drills causing the Khaki man, presumably, Mr. Martinez, to nearly jog to catch up with him.

"Sheriff Horne, I'm Sam Martinez. What can I do for you?" He held his hand out for the Sheriff.

The sniper's voice whispered in Ezra's earpiece,

"Sheriff, it looks to me like that cliff face is wired to blow. I don't know what's in the holes, but there appears to be Primacord strung all over the face."

Ezra ignored the outstretched hand and looked up the wall. His guy was right, the wall was liberally strewn with detonation cord of some sort

"Well Sam, you can start by telling me what the hell you guys are doing here?"

"We're working on an infrastructure project for the Town of Genna."

"Genna? You do realize that the town was all but destroyed on Thursday, don't you?"

"That is my understanding, although I have not witnessed it firsthand."

"Most of the county is shut down. Thirty thousand are homeless. A town is gone. Yet, two and a half days later, here you are working on an infrastructure project? Do you see why I might have a little trouble connecting the dots on this? What kind of 'infrastructure' are you building?"

Sam put on his smooth-talker facade, "Look, Sheriff, I understand how it might look. We are under contract, so despite the fire, not holding up my end of the bargain puts me in both legal and financial jeopardy. So we persevere. I assure you that all of my permits are in place. I just received the last of them on Wednesday morning."

Ezra looked over his shoulder, all of the site security appeared to be within ten yards of them. Most were not in an alert posture, in fact, most had their rifles slung across their backs. "Can you guys give us a little space? A little privacy to chat?"

"Sorry Sheriff, our job is to protect the site and Mr. Martinez." The muscular man in the middle of the pack replied. He had the bearing of a leader. The name tag on his uniform simply read, 'Sarge' though Ezra doubted that was his real name.

"Fine. Hey you guys don't know anything about a hiker that went missing early this morning, do you?"

"No, Sir." Came a dozen or more voices in unison.

"That's just weird"

"How so?" Asked Mr. Martinez.

"Because somehow with all this security, and I mean massive amounts of security for a construction site, you are asking me to believe that someone snuck into your secure camp and zip-tied a random hiker, whom none of you apparently saw either, to that bulldozer right over there." He pointed at the dozer. "Mr. Martinez, I am not sure what you are paying these boys but I suggest that you make a change."

"Who are you callin' boy?" Sarge said, with a face that expressed his personal offense.

"Each and every one of you, if this is the level of security that you provide." Intentionally poking at them, trying to get a reaction. And their undivided attention.

"Another interesting report from Thursday morning was of a second origin point of the fire." He gazed up the cliff pointing to a spot on the far-right lip from where they stood.

"Right about there."

He looked back at the group that had inched even closer.

"You guys wouldn't have had anything to do with that, would you?"

Sarge kept his poker face until he stole a glance over at Martinez. That was his tell. It told the Sheriff that he was asking permission to up the ante, which was exactly what the Sheriff was pushing for.

Martinez was pale. This was an action that he really didn't want to take, but he looked like he was ready to make a call. Ezra decided to give them one more push.

Still, in a congenial tone that spoke of his relaxed, unruffled confidence, he said, "Well, boys. Why don't you all drop your weapons? I am shutting this project down until we get some answers."

Martinez nodded his head ever so slightly, Sarge reacted instantly. He strode into Ezra's personal space, drawing his handgun as he approached. Sarge was intense but stupidly played his cards exactly as the Sheriff had intended. "I drop my weapon for no man." He got right into the Sheriff's face and every human eye within the project site watched closely to see how this played out.

"I had heard you were tough, but coming out here alone was dumb. Heavy equipment makes the body disposal a piece of cake. Sheriffs fit in the same size hole as anyone else. You drop your weapon and get your hands on your head!"

Martinez smiled, "Okay, enough fun and games. Sarge, take care of..." his words trailed off as he noticed Ezra's trump card being played.

More than thirty fully-outfitted S.W.A.T team members had materialized out of thin air while the Sheriff had attracted everyone's attention. They had surrounded the outnumbered guards silently. The need for silence had come to an end.

"Get on the ground, now!" bellowed the team leader's voice, causing everyone to whirl around. Hands instinctively reached for weapons as they spun, but survival instincts overrode that thought as they saw the force arrayed against them. Hands quickly shot into the air.

Hands quickly disarmed them and forced them onto their bellies. Sarge wasn't ready to concede just yet. He spun around behind the Sheriff with blinding speed and lifted his weapon toward Ezra's head. Ezra nodded almost imperceptibly. A fraction of a second later Sarge's elbow exploded in a puff of red and his handgun fell harmlessly to the ground, the sniper's bullet hitting its mark and quickly ending the intended standoff.

Epilogue

Two weeks later - Genna, ID

On the sixteenth day after the fire began, rain fell like manna from heaven, helping the fire crews to finally snuff the fire that had now burned over one-hundred-fifty thousand acres. Luckily, it hadn't seriously threatened any communities since day two. The destruction of Genna had taken a toll, on everyone.

The displaced population had overwhelmed Rome's services and shelters. Even restaurants had run out of food in the first few days of the aftermath, though they were beginning to find their balance as far as inventory went. The pre-fire housing shortage in the area, combined with the massive influx of the newly 'unhomed', had led to a massive spike in home prices and even rental rates, as some took advantage of the situation. Genna's residents had begun to scatter to places of safety with friends and family across the state and throughout the country.

Genna's residents were still barred from entering the town, causing a great deal of frustration amongst the masses. People were eager to find out the status of their homes and businesses.

Sam Martinez and his men faced a variety of charges, both at the federal and state level. It turned out that they had developed no actual plans for the sewer system. They were simply going to mine the enormous gold vein under the Ridge. The explosive charges had been rigged far too deeply into the rocky face to fly with their stated intent to shear off and smooth the wall to make it more suitable for sewer pipe attachment.

The gold beneath Genna is what justified, in their minds at least, such a security force.

Ironically, neither Sam Martinez nor any of the security guys below the Ridge had any knowledge of DJ and Bud's arson spree atop the Ridge, though they were intimately related.

No, that plan had been launched by Assistant Town Manager Marcus Moyer. He had been tasked by Jillian Dupree to "get the job done" and acquire the property rights. In his eagerness to grasp power he had overreached by a long shot. DJ and Bud had cut a deal with prosecutors and phone records had linked Marcus to the plot. He was being held without bail as he awaited a trial date. He was shooting for a plea deal for giving up dirt on Gavin David. Mr. David's private jet had disappeared over international waters just two days before. He is presumed to be dodging prosecution, but they were confident that he would surface sooner or later.

Jillian Dupree had resigned over the outrage against her office. There were still likely some charges that would eventually be filed against her, but for now, she had lost the confidence of the public. Not to mention, the ire of Interim Mayor Joshua Florini. Joanna Moody's connection to the deal, all done without Council approval, had cost her mayoral seat. She was still on the Town Council, but a movement to recall the entire council in a special election was gaining momentum quickly.

None of that mattered to James, at the moment anyway. He stood solemnly in the drizzle and watched the ash that had once been his home turn into some bizarre gray sludge within the footprint of his house. There was nothing left, save a couple of ceramic pieces and a few things made of steel. Everything else was ash. Loose nails littered the property, glass had melted out of the windows and the back patio table.

He could see his steel bed frame protruding from the ash, small puddles of aluminum elsewhere had gathered into strangely beautiful mini sculptures.

James wasn't mourning the loss of stuff. People, perhaps, but not stuff. Sixteen days prior he had been intimately engaged in his community... a community that had now scattered to the wind. It had been one of the best times of his life. But that life was over.

No, he wasn't mourning. He was facing the reality of what was, head-on. He was contemplating what his next move might be. Where would he go? What would he do? He had prayed multiple times per day asking for guidance but hadn't heard anything in response.

That was part of the reason that he had come up to Genna today. To face the magnitude of the destruction. But also, to find a peace and quiet, within his own head, that would allow him to hear guidance from the universe, from his God, from Mother Nature.

At that moment words appeared in his mind, not his words he was certain, they had come from somewhere else. But they were perfect. He said them out loud.

"Only by losing everything, do I gain the freedom to build a life of uncluttered purpose."

That was the answer and the proper mindset for him to be able to move forward.

Now he just had to identify what that purpose might be.

The End

Fact vs Fiction

On November 8th, 2018 a small fire broke out in a canyon near Pulga, in the mountains of Northern California. The nearest road was called Camp Creek Road, so the fire, due to naming conventions, was dubbed the #CampFire. Still the dumbest name for a wildfire imaginable. Because of it, much of the nation's population erroneously believes that it was started by an unattended campfire.

Due to a combination of drought, high winds, and poorly managed forest fuels, it took only a few hours for the flames to reach and virtually destroy the Town of Paradise, California. It also burnt the smaller communities of Concow, Pulga, Centerville, and parts of Magalia before turning out into the forested wildlands. It would go on to burn over 153,000 acres. In Paradise, it destroyed more than 12,000 homes and 2,000 businesses, displacing all of the 26,000 residents. It also claimed (officially) 88 lives. That combination of numbers makes it the most destructive and deadliest wildfire in California history.

I wanted to tell our story, and it was originally intended to be a non-fiction book. But as I began to write, I realized the truth. The truth was that our story had no ending, yet. Thousands were still homeless; couch surfing, living in tents, cars, motorhomes, fifth wheels and a handful in FEMA trailers even eight or nine months after that fateful day.

However, there were a great many conspiracy theories surrounding both the cause of the fire and the months-long ban on residents returning to Paradise.

So, I settled on fiction, weaving the story with more than twenty very real survivor stories (including my own) and some of the conspiracy theory storylines: gold, corruption, government land grabs, etc. Sorry guys, I chose to leave out the theories about alien lasers from space starting the fire (yes, some believe this).

Since the #CampFire recovery process is an on-going concern, I needed to make sure that these storylines were not confused with reality. So, I changed locations and names. I found a ridge in west-central Idaho that had much the same shape and many of the same features as the ridge that Paradise sits on.

The Maltese word for Paradise is, you guessed it, Genna. The fire itself also needed a dumb name to stay in character from the farcical reality, so in the book, it began off Bonneville Road and became known as the #BonnFire.

So, what is real? The vast majority of the fire and evacuation scenes were taken from first-person accounts of survivors, more than twenty people shared their stories with me for inclusion. I changed names and locations, combined some, used just chunks of others and took a bit of literary license with the rest. My aim was to take you into the fire, as deeply as words are able to express about such a surreal experience.

The appearance of the firenado was fictional, but there had been one outside of town during the #CarrFire near Redding, California several months before the #CampFire. I lifted the idea from that and placed it in the center of Genna simply because it is a phenomenon that is both horrifying and fascinating. The scene that had evacuees camped out at Walgreens is true. It happened. However, all of the side stories of what occurred inside were merely fictional. The Sheriff's daughter is indeed a Paradise Police officer, but I have no knowledge that she was at Walgreens.

All of the corruption, gold mining and involvement of the local government in any of it are fictional, but the debate and obsession over the sewer project is real.

One of the more subtle components that some beta-readers had questioned is, what happened to Holly and Hailey and Eric and the other characters that had been integral to the early part of the story and yet, were never mentioned again once they got off the hill. This is the reality of a disaster of this scope. Many people who survived the evacuation, unable to find hotels or lodging simply kept driving to their nearest relatives' house, friend's home whether that was fifty miles or two thousand miles, rarely to be seen again. People scatter and find a safe shelter wherever they can. I wrote an article called, *The Aftermath: A Community Scattered*, for Silver Sage Magazine at the six-month point after the fire that spelled out the numbers, demographics and geographic migration of #Campfire survivors.

Check it out if you want to know more https://wordsmithmojo.com/the-aftermath-a-community-scattered/

Thank You for taking the time to read, *BURN SCAR*.

If you enjoyed this novel, please leave it a review on Amazon. Reviews make a huge difference in the success of any new author and/or project.

With three more books currently in the works, there will be much more coming down the pike over the next year or so. To stay informed please sign up for my newsletter and you will get notifications of new releases. Don't worry, I hate spam as much as you do I will only occasionally send you something, and it will always be relevant: https://wordsmithmojo.com/newsletter/

Also, find and follow me here:

https://TJTaoBooks.com

https://www.facebook.com/TJTaoBooks/

https://twitter.com/TJTaoBooks/

BURN SCAR

CPSIA information can be obtained
at www.ICGtesting.com
Printed in the USA
FSHW010629041119
63719FS